THE PARALLEL CONGRESS

First edition, November 2016

This work is licensed under the Creative Commons Attribution-NonCommercial-ShareAlike 3.0 Unported License.

ISBN 978-1-537-61098-6

THE PARALLEL CONGRESS

TIM PARISE

The Maui Company
Maui, Hawaii

The famous cherry blossoms were long gone from the pillared lobby of the Willard Hotel. The palms, however, were flourishing in spite of the near-freezing temperatures outside. At the desk, a shell-shocked clerk hovered over a computer screen, not wanting to look up but forced to do so lest she be guilty of inadvertently neglecting a guest. Her shoulders slumped in relief as she saw the man cross the foyer away from her, towards the main entrance. In a far corner, a rumpled political operative who reeked of stale coffee and tobacco was jabbering into his phone in whispers. He'd be due for a coronary any time now, the observer thought with a trace of smug contempt for the campaigner and all that he represented. He allowed himself to pause and gloat for exactly ten seconds. Then he moved on, sweeping up a *Post* from one of the ornate tables spaced across the marble floor.

Underneath the blackletter masthead, the dateline read "Tuesday, November 3, 2020." Election Day.

"Mr. Soren! Mr. Soren!"

Alexander Soren grinned, and it took five years off his already youthful appearance. Two men were darting across the street towards him, dodging traffic, or rather allowing the traffic to dodge them. Shrieking brakes and horns broke the city's uncommon silence for a few moments before the pair of runners reached the hotel's entrance and the din died away.

"Only two of you? I thought there'd be more."

"You're hard to keep track of," the older journalist said, blowing like a walrus. His moustache heightened his resemblance to a large sea mammal. "Everyone thought you'd be in Palm Beach until this morning, and then you'd fly up for the opening ceremony."

"But you brought a colleague with you? How thoughtful of you."

"Not by choice. He wouldn't leave me alone." The *Post* glowered at the *New York Daily News,* who scowled back.

"Ah, I see. Rather than trail me, he trailed someone he thought could find me. Very nice. Efficient. Streamlined. But even so, I hate to disappoint you both. I've already chosen my morning reading." He waved the *Post* under their noses.

"Ha, ha," the reporter said, pretending to go along with the joke. "But seriously, would you care to comment on--"

"No chance. You can wait till the press conference--the opening ceremony, if you want to call it that, though I detect a hint of facetiousness in your use of the term--like everyone else. But," he added, raising a hand to silence their objections, "I'll give you something else you can use. If you behave yourselves."

"Okay. What is it?"

"Call a cab and I'll show you."

The New York man practically threw himself into the street and in front of a passing taxi. The driver leaned out the window and showered him with abuse in two languages. Ignoring his expletives, the reporters piled into the rear of the vehicle. Soren followed them more sedately.

"Best Buy," he ordered. "Just head up Fourteenth Street." The two journalists looked at him, confused.

"You were expecting something more dramatic?"

"Well, yeah."

"You are so readily disappointed. Here I am, about to give you a chance not only to witness the making of history, but to participate in it, and you complain. You are, to paraphrase Sayers, ghouls and cannibals."

"May I quote you on that?" the *Daily News* reporter asked, extending his phone. Soren shook his head gently and devoted himself to the *Post*'s editorial page, ignoring every question and remark that his fellow passengers made. He didn't look up until the cab squeaked to a halt in front of the store.

"Wait, please," he said to the driver, and stepped out. The reporters followed in his wake.

Inside, he came to a stop in the middle of a display of laptop computers and looked around.

"Can we help you?" the *Post* man asked, with heavy irony.

"Yes, actually," Soren replied. "Pick out one of these computers for me."

"Any of them?"

"Any one that comes with Linux preinstalled will do, yes."

The journalist blinked, scanned the labels, and settled on a Dell machine as the most familiar choice. "How's that?"

"Perfect. Now, if you would be so good as to take it up to the counter and pay for it, I'd be very grateful."

"Lost your wallet?"

The corners of Soren's mouth twitched. "You'll see. In a couple of hours I think you'll be very grateful to me for this stunt. Besides, your expense account can stand the strain."

The *Post* grumbled but complied. The *Daily News* edged up beside Soren. "Anything I can get for you?"

"Certainly. The cab fare."

Back in the taxi, Soren failed to become any more communicative. In desperation, one of the reporters pulled up CNN on his phone.

"...and of course the big story this Election Day," the anchor was saying, "is the new project by philanthropist Alexander Soren: the 'Parallel Congress', as he calls it. Now, we all complain about Congress, especially if we happen to live in the District, but somehow Soren's solution to its problems never occurred to any of us. If Congress breaks, why not replace it with something new?

"Soren isn't actually suggesting that we replace Congress. Not yet, anyway. But he is suggesting that we replace its members. The Parallel Congress, he said in the only public statement that he has made so far, is a social experiment designed to demonstrate what a truly democratic decision-making body would look like. It will be composed entirely of citizens selected at random from the general population of the United States. And he intends to bring these parallel congressmen and senators to Washington for two years, to supply them with all the paraphernalia of elective office, and see what decisions they make and what laws they pass. As such, he intends it to act as an example to and a commentary on the actions of the real Congress. Estimates for the cost of this experiment have run into the hundreds of millions of dollars, casting serious doubt on whether Soren will be able to afford to complete it.

"Political activists of all stripes have uniformly condemned the Parallel Congress, both on the grounds that it will disrupt the actual proceedings of Congress, and on the grounds that it will encourage an ill-advised movement towards popular participation in government. Two-time Democratic presidential contender Senator Mike Gravel, known for his support for introducing referenda on a national scale, has dismissed Soren's proposal as 'futile'."

"They're not exactly giving you a fair hearing," the *Daily News* commented. "Lessig said it was a nice idea." Soren merely shrugged. Lawrence Lessig, a professor who had twice sought the Democratic presidential nomination on the single issue of electoral reform, produced too much heartburn in those who thought that the Constitution was a sacred document for him to be given much airtime.

The clip on the screen flashed to an interview with former UN ambassador and perennial Republican candidate Alan Keyes. "The exercise of responsible judgment," Keyes was saying, "is an essential aspect of the contribution that citizens make to the purpose of elections, and that elections make to the character required for citizenship. Leaving it to chance would eliminate that contribution. It would eliminate the deliberative aspect of representation, transforming our form of government into a pure democracy, a form much more likely to degenerate into tyranny."

Next up was Susan Herman, president of the ACLU, who was flinging her words over her shoulder as she walked away from the interviewer. "We do not take a position on the Parallel Congress," she said dismissively. "We have more than enough to do defending the Constitution's guarantees of rights and equal protection of the laws."

"Ouch," the *Post* remarked.

A co-chair of the Green Party made a brief plea in favor of proportional representation and ranked choice voting. Next came author Warren Farrell, who was more vehement in his opposition to the suggestion that selecting Congress from the general population would be an improvement over elections. "It deprives the people of responsibility; and the average representative is much smarter and more thoughtful than the average person," he argued. Dr. Tom Stevens, chair of the Objectivist Party, agreed. "Elected representatives at least have people who voted for them based on their promises. Those elected at random might be incompetent, uninterested in serving, criminals and simply would not have a mandate. In a representative republic, the people must vote to elect the representatives of their choice."

"Would you still not care to comment?" the *Daily News* inquired, closing the feed.

"Shortly," Soren said, reaching for the handle of the door.

They stepped out of the cab into a circle of screaming journalists and broadcasters. The clicking of cameras blurred into a steady noise in the background that recalled the wings of locusts. Boom mikes hung overhead like spongy fungi dangling from the ceiling of an invisible cavern. The organizing committee of the Parallel Congress had clearly put no effort at all into press relations; Anderson Cooper and Katie Couric could be seen struggling in the herd along with every little political blogger in DC. Half a dozen security guards, noticing their arrival, began making a path through the crowd.

"With me," Soren said, abruptly snapping out of his cultivated apathy. He was through the press pack in seconds and into the building. The two reporters were practically forced after him by the pressure of their colleagues and competitors.

"Where exactly are we?" the *Post* demanded.

"The selection offices of the Parallel Congress, on Constitution Avenue." The reporters looked around and were startled to see the Capitol dome looming over them from across the street.

"You've got good taste in headquarters. Very...suggestive."

"Thank you. It seemed an appropriate location. This way, please." He led them towards a pair of double doors that were the only obvious exit from the foyer.

"Good lord," one of them gasped, halting a pace through the doorway. "What are you trying to do here, recreate the War Room?"

"The War Room does not exist."

"Then you've put a lot of effort into creating it."

They were standing in a two-story ballroom, or at least in a single great room that had been knocked together from a number of smaller office suites. It was draped in black and unlit except for the pale autumn light that leaked in from the windows of the second-floor gallery, which occupied the space above the foyer they had just left. Most of the floor was empty space. No chairs, no carpets, no cameras. At the far end, a low dais ran along the rear wall, with stainless steel staircases running up to the gallery from its extremities. Above it were three large projection screens, the outer two angled inwards. The front of the platform was occupied by a single table with cables running to it, and behind them extended a row of consoles, all lit up, all manned by operators with headsets. Above the workers, footage of the ongoing elections played out on the three screens.

"Who do you plan to nuke first?" the *Daily News* asked jovially. "And where's the red button?"

"He's carrying it." Soren nodded at the *Post*, who nearly dropped the computer he'd been lugging with him. "If you two would stand over here?" He escorted them onto the platform and motioned them to seats off to one side. A member of his staff ran up and conferred with him as he took his Burberry off. Half a dozen other men and women drifted onto the dais. At last Soren nodded.

"All right. Let them in."

The chaos from outside poured into the foyer and flooded the auditorium. Everywhere reporters were battling for position while their camera crews fought for the best vantage points. The floor filled; so did the gallery. Soren stood behind the table, looking down at them all with unconcern. Gradually they shouted themselves hoarse and settled down of their own accord. The object of their attention straighted one of his cuffs and finally moved to the front of the platform.

"Good morning. My name is Alexander Soren." His voice was amplified by a tiny headset instead of the traditional podium and microphone.

"Today, I will oversee the selection of the First Parallel Congress of the United States.

"Many of you, or the organizations you represent, or the editorial writers with whom you are associated"--that got a murmur of denial from the crowd--"have been asking, since I formally announced this project six months ago, for details about it which I did not provide in my statement to the press, and criticizing me for not being more forthcoming. Those details I have withheld intentionally, until today. Let me begin by reminding you of the point of this experiment: to contrast the actions of a government of the people with those of a government elected by the people. The semantic difference between those two phrases is subtle; the implementation of them is drastically different, as we shall soon see.

"One of the talking heads on the news this morning was saying, and I quote, 'we all complain about Congress.' Would we complain as much about Congress, I wonder, if that Congress were composed of ourselves? But how would we select such a Congress with utter impartiality? The most reasonable answer is that we would not do it at all. A computer would undertake that part of the task.

"In 1952, the UNIVAC I computer shocked the political world by accurately predicting an Eisenhower victory in the presidential election based on poll results from one percent of voters. Three years later, Isaac Asimov penned a short story, "Franchise", that explored the role computers might play in the elections of the future if their deductive abilities continued to grow.

"Asimov's story is part of his Multivac series, in which many of the activities of mankind are organized or coordinated by a sentient computer called Multivac. "Franchise" is set early in the cycle, when Multivac has taken over the management of elections, but not of government itself. On Election Day, it selects from its databases a single voter, one whom it considers to be the most typical specimen of an American citizen, and interviews him, asking him trivial questions and measuring his responses exactly. Then, from those responses, Multivac accurately predicts the result of every election in the United States, from the presidency down to city councils and school boards, without a ballot ever being cast. Elections in the traditional sense have been outmoded because it can anticipate and simulate their outcomes.

"Obviously Asimov was an optimist. We have no computer that has improved on UNIVAC to such an extent, and we never will. Nor should we wish to. For anyone, human or machine, to tell us how we would have voted would be an act of intolerable condescension. However, the Multivac story did suggest to me a way in which we might use a computer to select our officials. If we cannot rely on it to make intelligent decisions, we can at least expect it to make effectively random ones. If we fed into it the names of all American citizens, we could ask it to give us five hundred names at random, and we could so arrange that those five hundred men and women, selected by lot, should constitute our government. Direct democracy might be unwieldy in a nation of three hundred millions, but it would be a great deal more likely if our representatives were drawn from the general population instead of from a small, aristocratic, self-selecting group.

"You will naturally say that the Constitution does not provide for such a method of selecting representatives. To that I answer that the Constitution has already been amended to alter the process by which the Senate is elected. It was done once, and it can be done again for Congress as a whole. But to generalize is not to explain." Soren removed a single sheet of paper from the breast pocket of his coat and unfolded it. "Here is what such an amendment might look like." He read the draft aloud:

"Section One. Clauses one through four of Section 2, clauses one through three of Section 3, and clause one of Section 4 of Article One of the Constitution of the United States are hereby repealed, together with the Seventeenth Amendment.

"Section Two. The House of Representatives shall be composed of five hundred Members chosen by lot every second year from among all citizens of the United States eligible to vote, by an officer appointed by the House of Representatives for that purpose.

"Section Three. The Senate of the United States shall be composed of two Senators from each State, chosen by lot every six years from among all citizens of each State eligible to vote, by an officer appointed by the Senate for that purpose, and each Senator shall have one vote.

"Section Four. Should any person chosen as a Representative or a Senator decline to serve, or should a vacancy occur in the membership of either the House of Representatives or the Senate, the responsible officer shall select by lot a replacement to fill the resulting vacancy for the remainder of the Congressional term.

"Section Five. Should a person be chosen as both a Representative and a Senator at the same time, he shall be permitted to choose which office he desires to hold, at which time the responsible officer of either the House of Representatives or the Senate shall select by lot a replacement to fill the office the original nominee has declined.

"Section Six. Congress may at any time specify the time, place, and manner of the selection of Representatives and Senators." He returned the paper to his pocket.

"If this document were approved by Congress and the states, it would become the Twenty-Eighth Amendment. This is the assumption that underlies our experiment: that such an amendment has become law and provides the constitutional framework necessary to permit the Parallel Congress to assemble.

"The amendment as proposed is fairly straightforward. Random selection of members of both houses from the general population; empty seats to be filled in the same manner; no person can hold seats in both houses at once; the House to be expanded to an even five hundred seats, since that is a more rational number and will allow membership to be statistically more representative of the general population. Legal scholars will note that it says nothing about preserving the language regarding direct taxes that appears in Article One, Section 2, Clause Three, since that provision is repeated later in Section 9, Clause Four. Since the amendment does not abolish voting in state and local election, it uses the criterion of voter eligibility to determine eligibility for Congressional selection.

"In actual practice, it might provide a better balance to continue to have the Senate elected while the House was selected by lot. In this experiment, though, that would not be possible, since we cannot convincingly run half a Congress. Therefore, the draft amendment I have just presented to you was written to cover both. It could easily be altered to apply to only the lower house if that was considered desirable. After all, what is the point of a bicameral legislature if both houses are chosen by the same electorate?

"One thing that the amendment does not specify is the rate of pay for members of the Parallel Congress. That is a deliberate omission to refrain from complicating its theoretical passage. Members of the Parallel Congress, while they serve, will receive annual salaries equal to the total income that they reported on their previous year's taxes. They will not receive the same inflated pay that their elected counterparts do.

"Now, as to its implementation. We cannot choose the Parallel Congress from among all Americans; we do not have such an extensive database as the government does, and it would increase our difficulties to be dropping down on people who have never heard of us to ask them if they would like to participate in our experiment. Instead, over the past three years, we have built a smaller database of our own, from which we will select our six hundred members. It contains two million names instead of two hundred and fifty million. These names have been collected by volunteers for the purpose of this experiment. We have taken great care to ensure that the number of participants in each state and major city are proportional to the population of those states and cities. Within those limits, we have recruited at random until we had a sufficient number of respondents. Every one of the individuals we have registered has agreed, when signing up, to serve in the Parallel Congress if selected. That will cut down the time we spend on confirming members significantly.

"That, I think, will give you a fair idea of how the Parallel Congress will function. But it does not answer the question of why I decided that this experiment was necessary or useful.

"I keep thinking back to what I heard this morning. 'We all complain about Congress.' It was such a simple statement of fact, one that didn't show any need to prove itself. We take for granted that our political system is dysfunctional and our officials, both elected and appointed, are corrupt. They are only politicians, we say. They can't help themselves. They have to be like that to get elected.

"And therein lies the solution. If they were not elected, and could not expect to have long and profitable careers in government, their incentives to be corrupt and compromising would disappear. If the members of Congress, a few weeks before their selection, had been working ordinary jobs and living ordinary lives, they would not be so detached from reality as are those who make getting into power their profession. But even they are almost victims in a sense. We have created an electoral system that forces would-be leaders into a narrow mold, and voters to select from essentially identical candidates in many cases. We have raised up an elected aristocracy without actually admitting it. There are masses of data available on just how unrepresentative Congress is. To pick two statistics alone, fully half of the members of Congress are millionaires; just over three percent of Americans as a whole are. You are one hundred and five times more likely to find a Harvard graduate among members of Congress than you are among the general population. And these are only a couple of the most egregious differences. How can a body skewed so far from the demographic average truly call itself representative of the people? It cannot. A Congress chosen from among the people--as the

Parallel Congress will demonstrate--would not face that problem.

"Another factor to consider is the financial merit of abolishing elections. We spent over seven billion dollars on them in 2012 and over ten billion in 2016. This year, they cost more than twelve billion. I may point out that this is more than the entire annual budget for fifteen different states as well as for one hundred and five different countries. Whether you complain about taxes being too high or government spending being too low, there are unquestionably better uses for the volumes of public and private money being poured into the promotion of worthless candidates for public office.

"And now, ladies and gentlemen, I will take your questions."

For perhaps ten seconds there was a hush in the room before someone stepped forward.

"Isn't the right to vote a fundamental human right? And isn't taking it away from people a blow to democracy, rather than an improvement?"

"The right to vote? From what can you deduce that?" Soren demanded. "There is unquestionably a right to participate in one's government, yes, but how that is interpreted depends on the form of government one has. It may involve voting. It may involve, in a functioning democracy, actually participating in the making of laws. It may involve approving laws already passed by a legislative body. It may merely involve revolting and deposing the king or president every few centuries. Twentieth-century scholars have been at great pains to make participation seem synonymous with voting, but it is far from being the only method available. As for democracy, have you ever tried calling your congressman? If you have, and you had a request to make, has he ever bothered to listen to you? I would assume the answer in both cases would be no. The argument for keeping elected representatives would be that they hear all the voices of their constituents and can represent them all in the deliberations of the state--but in the real world, they hear none of them. In fact, they purposefully ignore them. So if your voice is going to be ignored anyway, it is far more democratic for some of the population to have a voice than none. And how is a right to serve in your country's government if called upon to do so somehow less participatory than a right to delegate someone else to serve?"

"How do you expect political parties to be represented in the Parallel Congress?"

"I don't. Since members will not be dependent on a party for their selection, they will have no reason to have strong ties to a party. Oh, they may form informal voting blocs at first, but those will fall apart relatively quickly. The true political leanings of the American people are adequately encapsulated by none of the existing parties, since a party by definition is organized around an ideology, and an ideology need not take reality into consideration." The way he said that got him a chuckle from the audience. "Bear in mind that fewer than thirty percent of Americans consider themselves to be Democrats, and about the same number consider themselves to be Republicans. The remainder differ substantially from either of the major parties. This is a significant advantage of the random selection method, in fact: it will work to eliminate political parties and their associated cronyism without having to resort to the anti-democratic method of banning or regulating them."

"But how will you get laws passed and avoid deadlock without party labels around which members can organize themselves?"

"Very simply. If a bill does not have the necessary support to move forward, it will die. Only measures with general support can be passed. There will be no more arm-twisting behind the scenes, no three-line whips, as the British put it. No party discipline of any kind, which impairs the representatives' ability to represent the mass of the people. No minority group will be able to shut down the government, block action, or force a bill through by calling in favors. Parties do not aid governance; they hinder it. Party government is tantamount to handing two or three competing cliques the reins of power and disregarding everyone who is not a member of one of those groups. It is highly undemocratic, and the sooner we get rid of it, the better. With any luck, the Parallel Congress will set the United States and the rest of the world a good example."

"For the past few election cycles, a lot of voters and independent candidates have been calling for term limits on members of Congress, but Congress has refused to take up the question. Your amendment does not address it, either."

"That is because term limits are unnecessary under the random selection system. The chance of any person being selected for two terms in the Parallel Congress is one in four trillion. In the real Congress, which would be drawn from a much larger population, the probability would be one in sixty-two and a half quadrillion. In other words, it will never happen. Should it happen, it would be almost a guarantee that the selection process had been rigged somehow. Representatives and senators alike will serve one term, a brief hiatus out of their ordinary careers, and then return to private life. The elected aristocracy, where members serve as legislators for twenty or thirty years and then hand over their seats to hand-groomed successors from the same background and with the same training, will cease to exist. The career politician will be abolished, together with his connections in the government and the civil service. So will his golden parachute, the highly-paid teaching and consulting and lobbying jobs that come inevitably to retired members of Congress. Since all of his colleagues will have retired at the same time that he did, he will have no influence to peddle and will be worthless to lobbyists and corporations. No more revolving doors between the houses of Congress and private industry. The influence of money on our political system would be diminished overnight.

"I should add that it would be further diminished by the elimination of elections. The furor over political action committees and campaign spending would end at once. If there are no candidates at all, it is impossible to bribe the candidates of your choice. So would the problems of gerrymandering, with eligibility being determined on a national basis rather than depending on districts drawn by the party in power to give themselves an advantage. Really, the only argument for having kept elections around this long, considering how poorly they have served us throughout our history, is blind obedience to tradition."

"Your amendment also omits the age limits specified for senators and representatives in the Constitution. Are we to assume that is intentional?"

"You are. Age limits are highly undemocratic. They are equivalent to telling the young that they have nothing to contribute to their country's welfare. The age requirements originally written into the Constitution have been responsible for one of the largest demographic distortions in the membership of Congress. Citizens between the ages of twenty and twenty-nine comprise fourteen percent of the population and exactly zero percent of congressmen. The situation is almost as bad in the thirty to thirty-nine age group. American legislators are overwhelmingly older than their constituents, and thus more reactionary and inflexible. This creates the awkward case of a population that is intellectually and emotionally far ahead of its lawmakers and its laws. In fact, the distortion is so extreme that the Constitution's age limits are irrelevant. They were designed to keep the inexperienced out, but the two-party system has arranged matters so that only candidates with extensive resumes stand a real chance, and those resumes take so long to build that candidates are well past the age limit by the time they can mount a practical campaign. By drawing its membership at random from all voting-age citizens, the Parallel Congress will avoid this problem. Its senators and representatives will represent the ages of the population from which they are drawn, in approximately the same proportions found in the United States as a whole."

"Do you mean that it will have--going by your numbers--more than eighty members under the age of thirty?"

"That is correct."

"You are selling this Parallel Congress project as an experiment in democracy. How do you account for the fact that so many prominent political figures have come out against it. Doesn't that prove that it is undemocratic?"

Soren cocked his head to one side. "In which way? Because bastions of democracy have called it undemocratic, therefore it is? Or because a majority of those you interviewed have called it undemocratic, period--the argumentum ad populatum? In either case, the objection is unwarranted. You're asking the wrong people. The names I heard on CNN this morning were hardly what any objective journalist would call unbiased sources. They were all either candidates, present or former, or people with an agenda they wished to promote. They are in the business of politics either because they want to make a good thing out of it for themselves, or because they have a viewpoint which they wish to impose on the rest of the country. Their only chance to accomplish those goals is to win seats in Congress by means of an election. Take away elections, put the legislative power in the hands of genuine popular representatives, and they no longer have jobs. They go extinct. They can never achieve their personal or ideological goals without a system that narrows the candidate pool to a number that they can control. Given that their own lifetime chances of selection to the Parallel Congress would be about one in five million, naturally they oppose the idea. All the more so because it's likely to be popular among the masses and thus would stand an actual chance of implementation in real life. It sends them into a fury to think of the missed opportunities. You are continually forgetting that these people are aristocrats, no matter whether they profess progressive or conservative views. They truly believe that they are the only ones qualified for or deserving of public office. The thought of the rabble intruding into government, a mob without connections, experience, or philosophy, nauseates them as much as it did the French nobility before the Revolution. My scheme offers them nothing. Why would they support it?

"And while I am addressing the opposition that the Parallel Congress project has faced, allow me to single out a few criticisms in particular that I think are worth rebutting. There are those who have claimed that selecting the government from among the people would let criminals into the government. Oh! criminals! How horrible! After all, there are no criminals in Congress already, right?" His audience exploded with laughter. "May I remind you that, on average, at least one member of Congress is convicted of a felony every year? But cynicism aside, are not criminals citizens as well, and do they not have a claim to exercise the rights of citizenship equal to that of any other group of citizens? An overwhelming majority of Americans support ending felon disenfranchisement--no doubt because it is so easy to be convicted of a crime today. Which is another point in favor of the random selection method, rather than one against it. If those who have been convicted of nonviolent crimes, or crimes against themselves, or crimes against the state, which is to say, the majority of all criminals in this country, are given a voice in government, maybe we will finally see substantial reforms to our legal system. Perhaps crimes will actually be taken off the books, rather than added to them.

"Then there is the claim that members of Congress are more competent and more intelligent than the average citizen. Tell me, exactly what evidence is there of this? We have congressmen who are so intelligent that they can't tell the difference between Sunni and Shia. We had a congressman who was so intelligent that he thought you could stop conception from happening by thinking about it hard enough. We have congressmen who are so intelligent that they don't realize that ice melts when it gets warm outside. Can the general population really be expected to contain many citizens even less intelligent than this? I doubt it.

"Finally, the question has been raised whether individuals with no experience in making or understanding laws--meaning the general public rather than the lawyer-heavy Congress--would be able to draft adequate laws for the nation. Not only am I confident that they can do so, I am sure it will be an advantage. They will be unable to design complex bills. All legislation will have to be simple and direct, so that it can be understood by the members, who will have to consider it as individuals rather than merely voting as directed by their party affiliations, and so that it can garner enough support to pass from the disparate factions existing withing the institution. There will be an end to laws that are little more than coded references to other laws. Again, the notion that only a select body of people is somehow qualified to design laws is a throwback to an aristocracy. There is nothing so inherently complex about legislation that it demands expert knowledge, and even if it did, the advantages gained by it are immaterial in comparison to the importance of democratic principles."

"Do you think that your proposed amendment would ever stand a real chance of becoming law?"

"No. The people might vote for it, but before it could be sent to the people it would have to be approved by Congress or demanded by the state legislatures. And not a single member of any of them would support the amendment, because if it succeeded, then goodbye to their careers and their entire philosophy of life."

"Then what's the point of your experiment?"

"To cast into high relief just how undemocratic the world's greatest democracy is. And to lead by example rather than by force, which is something that the United States has long forgotten how to do." Soren turned and glanced at a clock on the far wall. "It is now ten o'clock. If you have further questions, I will do my best to address them this afternoon. At the moment, we have a Parallel Congress to select."

He beckoned to the two reporters who had been following him around all morning. They joined him at the table.

"The gentleman from the *Washington Post*," Soren said, making sure that the cameras had an unobstructed view of him, "is holding the computer that will serve as our Multivac in this experiment. He purchased it this morning off the shelf. He did not know what purpose he was buying it for, and it has not left his possession since then. This is the sort of safeguard against tampering that would need to be formally instituted should the Twenty-Eighth Amendment ever be passed."

"So what do I do with it now?" the *Post* man asked.

"Start it up," Soren instructed him. One of the technicians left his console and connected a cable to the laptop. The three great screens above their heads went dark.

"As the computer is set up for the first time," Soren explained, "you will be able to follow every step of the process on the screens in front of you, as an additional safeguard. Every election, and more than ever in the last two, there are allegations of voter fraud because ballots are counted in secret and no one knows what kind of programming goes into electronic voting machines. In the case of the Parallel Congress, this is not possible. The selection process is simpler by design and therefore less likely to produce erroneous results. Moreover, it will take place publicly, under the eyes of dozens of witnesses. I should also point out what some of you have doubtless already noticed: that this room is shielded against electronic transmissions and that it is therefore unlikely that the machine can be hacked in the short amount of time available to a potential intruder."

The startup menus were flashing by on the screens as the journalist input the date and time zone and login information. "What are you going to use for a username?" someone in the crowd shouted.

The reporter swiveled around and looked at Soren. "How about Multivac?" he said.

"Why not?" the philanthropist shrugged. There was some faint applause from the rear of the room.

"And a password?"

"Anything you like. It will only be used once, so it doesn't matter."

The computer shut down and booted back up. The screens filled with an image of its desktop, new and uncluttered.

"Excellent," Soren said. He nodded in the direction of a young man behind the technicians, who came up to the table. Two uniformed security officers followed him.

"This is Mr. Brewster of Williams and Connolly, who has been responsible for the safekeeping of the database of Americans from which the Parallel Congress will be drawn." Brewster held up a USB drive and flashed a tight smile at the reporters. "The list of names, over two million in all, was placed in a safe deposit box one month ago, and he has only removed it within the last hour. Inspection of the bank's security footage would guarantee that it has not been tampered with, as will the guards who have been escorting it. Mr. Brewster?"

The lawyer plugged the drive into the computer. It opened automatically, showing a single folder, titled *Databases*, in its memory.

"Drop the folder onto the desktop and unplug the drive, please," Soren instructed. The *Post* did so. Brewster reappropriated the drive and retired into the background.

"We now have the data we require to make our selection, and all that is left is to run the appropriate commands," Soren continued. He stepped in front of the computer and the two journalists stood aside. Tapping the enter key, he opened the folder to reveal fifty-one text files. "As you can see, it is already sorted to simplify the process. One file contains the names of all participants; the others contain the names of those participants resident in each individual state. We will now run the larger file, which will give us our Parallel House."

Soren right-clicked on the folder and selected "Open Terminal Here". A new window popped up, plain white text on black, displaying the machine's username and the directory path. He typed in a command:

```
cat all.txt | sort -R | head
-500 > /home/multivac/Desktop/
parallelhouse.txt
```

Then he pressed enter once more. For thirty seconds the computer did nothing before blinking back to a ready command line again. He straightened up.

"Ladies and gentlemen, the five hundred members of the House of Representatives have been selected."

"Just like that?" a voice demanded.

"Just like that. Oh, certainly I could have had someone build a program that would have fed the names out to you dramatically, one at a time. But that would have been not only superfluous but risky. Every added layer of complexity is an opportunity for sabotage or manipulation of the selection process. By contrast, the command I just ran is built into every Linux system and is thus much safer. One can more easily choose a machine at random, or install a fresh operating system if necessary, if you can take advantage of the built-in tools within the basic programming." Soren minimized his open windows and double-clicked the new file on the desktop. A list of names filled all three screens.

"I am now going to scroll through this list while we record the names visually as a further safeguard. I expect you are doing so as well."

Cameras flashed. Journalists darted in and out of the room, compromising between their desire to tweet the names live and the reality that they couldn't get a signal inside the auditorium thanks to Soren's precautions. The list unfolded steadily before their eyes, almost without pause. The cameras were getting it all.

"Are the numbers after each name to prevent confusion?" a reporter near the front asked.

"Yes. For the real Congress, the respective houses would probably use Social Security numbers. For the Parallel Congress, we have assigned each participant a reference number." Soren reached the end of the list and closed it.

"In a few minutes I will transfer this list to our technicians, who will begin contacting the participants to ensure that they are willing to serve. First, however, to minimize the possibility that a virus could be introduced into the machine at the time of that connection, we will select the members of the Parallel Senate as well." He tapped the touchpad and the command line reappeared. "Watch closely, please," he advised the press. "You are the proctors of this election."

More commands followed, patterned after the first:

```
cat alabama.txt | sort -R | head
-2 > /home/multivac/Desktop/
Senate/alabama.txt
cat alaska.txt | sort -R | head -2
> /home/multivac/Desktop/Senate/
alaska.txt
cat arizona.txt | sort -R | head
-2 > /home/multivac/Desktop/
Senate/arizona.txt
```

...and so on, and so on, until Soren had run through all fifty states. He opened the new folder on the desktop that his commands had created. Fifty files filled it.

"Each of these contains the names of the two senators who will represent their states in the Parallel Senate. I will now show you these names as well before they are transferred."

It took eleven minutes for Soren to disclose the identities of the hundred senators. Behind him, his technicians were making frantic notes, getting ahead of the rush wherever possible. On the floor, the audience was torn between making a faithful record of the proceedings and trying to figure out who the selectees really were. If they could interview a future member of the Parallel Congress before the organizers had a chance to contact him, it would mean a scoop for them--but Soren's shielding was thwarting their efforts.

A technician came up with a new flash drive. He plugged it in, and Soren dropped all the files with the selectees' names onto it, then ejected it. He carried it back to his station and reopened it. The two outer screens switched to showing his terminal so the press could monitor his activities as he shared the files with his fellows. The middle screen changed to a roster of the membership of the Parallel Congress, as yet unfilled.

The technician could be seen to enter the reference number for the first name on the House list into his more complete database. It flashed green and gave him back a phone number. He pressed a key and nodded to Soren, who picked up a handset on top of the consoles. A moment later a ringtone filled the air, broadcast by speakers powerful enough to reach everyone in the audience.

Three rings, four rings. A click and background noise. "Hello?" a young woman's voice asked.

"May I speak to Margaret Proctor, please," Soren said.

"Yeah, one sec." The girl on the other end of the line screeched something unintelligible. There was the sound of the phone being fumbled, and then of a more mature voice in the distance. "Yes?"

"Is this Margaret Proctor?"

"It is."

"Mrs. Proctor, my name is Alexander Soren. I am the director of the Parallel Congress Project, which our records indicate that you signed up for at a previous date. Is that correct?"

"Yes, I believe so."

"I am pleased to tell you that you are the first person selected to hold a seat in the House of Representatives in the Parallel Congress, beginning on Inauguration Day in January. Are you still interested in serving?"

"Oh, my goodness. Yes...yes, I think so."

"Excellent. We will be contacting you within the next week to make the necessary arrangements. Thank you very much for your participation."

"Thank you for the opportunity."

"It is our pleasure. Have a wonderful Selection Day." Soren put the phone down. The speakers cut off, and the name of Margaret Proctor appeared at the head of the roster. The other two screens split into six sections, showing the terminals of the technicians as they began dialing the next set of names on the House list.

"And that," Soren announced, turning back to the press, "is the way an election should be conducted. Simple, efficient, and dignified. Open for everyone to see, since publicity is the surest safeguard. No screaming, no personalities, no emotions. Perfectly reasonable and democratic."

"Except that no one had a choice in the matter!" one reporter screamed.

"Which do you think the average American would prefer?" Soren retorted. "The great privilege of being able to choose between two nearly identical candidates, who at best would only share fifty percent of their views, or the knowledge that in a national random selection, dozens of ordinary people sharing exactly their views would be sitting in Congress helping to make the laws?" He stepped forward, carried away by his enthusiasm. "Now there's a choice for them to make! Give them that choice. Pass the amendment. I dare you to do so!"

The tension of the moment was broken by the voice of a computer journalist. "The commands you used did not produce perfectly random results."

"Correct. The algorithms used to generate the results are pseudorandom. However, in this case, the simpler process is just as statistically valid. We are not building an unbreakable code, after all, we are only picking names from a list. And as long as the operating system has not been tampered with, pseudorandom selection will produce usable results."

"But if greater randomness is desired--"

"Then you move to a physical rather than a digital system, like a lottery number generator. Lotteries, I should point out, operate under more stringent safeguards than do elections."

Behind him, the membership roster of the House was filling up. "Has anyone declined selection yet?"

Soren glanced at his technicians before responding. "One person so far."

"And you'll fill empty seats at the end by running the list again?"

"That is correct."

"And then what?"

"Then we make arrangements for them to come to Washington."

* * * * *

The cardinal looked at Soren, and then danced away across the snow, disappearing into a hedge with a flick of its scarlet wings. Its tracks were almost invisible on the hard crust by the edge of the sidewalk.

"Very appropriate," Soren said to no one in particular. He shoved his hands farther down in his pockets and started up the hill, being careful not to slip on the icy surface.

To his left, neat dormitories marched upwards in orderly stacks, a hint of San Francisco on the Potomac. Above them soared Gothic spires and brick facades more reminiscent of Edinburgh than the seat of American government which brooded farther downstream. The picture was complicated and deranged by the immense concrete structure on his right, a cascade of libraries and parking garages that was a triumph of Brutalism. And of cost-cutting as well, though no one really talked about that. It blocked the sun and cast an immense shadow over the lawn where the press would be assembled. A perfect winter day in the District of Columbia, without a single cloud to obstruct the radiance of what one talk show host had disparagingly called "a new dawn" that morning--and he had to cope with the shadows left behind by lesser intellects. "And that," he murmured, "is a metaphor for all of politics, and all of innovation as well. The trick of success is to avoid fixating on the messes your predecessors leave for you."

Ahead of him, bright parkas were bobbing up and down along Library Walk. With almost no obstruction from administrators, Georgetown University had agreed to cancel classes for the day, citing logistical and historical reasons. Soren expected half the student body to turn out to watch the seating of the Parallel Congress. Of course, it was an immense boon for the college to have the Parallel Congress meeting on its campus. The publicity alone was worth far more than the cost, and Soren's offer of a seven-figure contribution to the university's miniscule endowment had removed any lingering hesitation on the part of the board of directors. It would be a matchless teaching aid as well, the faculty had agreed. It would provide for the possibility of dozens, if not hundreds, of internships and other positions that could be filled by students. From Soren's point of view, Georgetown had three other advantages. It had the necessary space. It was an elegant environment with a past as old as the capital itself, touching the Parallel Congress with an aura of solidity that a rented commercial building would not have conferred. And, perhaps most importantly from a visual standpoint, it towered over the Capitol and the administrative buildings of downtown Washington. See, the Georgetown campus seemed to say, here we are, the people, and we wait only our moment to take what is rightfully ours back from you who are interlopers.

He chuckled. Ahead of him, the crowd was thickening. The parking lot outside the Riggs Library was filled with vans from local television and radio stations. Cables ran in every direction. Students and members of the public were jostling for position. The street was barricaded off, but the campus police guarding it recognized Soren and waved him through, practically coming to attention as he passed. The bystanders picked up on it. Cameras snapped. Oblivious to them for the time being, Soren paused and looked around in astonishment.

Healy Lawn was packed solid with spectators, even with the thermometer slightly below freezing. Temporary bleachers had been erected all over Healy Cirle and Copley Lawn, and 37th Street was closed to traffic for the entire block to provide additional standing room. The buildings fronting on it across from Healy boasted roofs filled with viewers. Soren counted twenty television cameras above their parapets before giving up the attempt as a waste of time. Inside the apartments, faces bobbed back and forth in front of the windows. It had been reported that students were throwing little Inauguration Day parties and serving coffee and cocoa to a lucky few who wanted to watch the Parallel Congress sworn in from the comfort of a warm room while still being able to claim that they'd been there in person. They wouldn't have a bad view, actually. Mostly of the bleachers in front of Healy, where the members of the Parallel Congress would be installed for the ceremony.

"Mr. Soren?" President DeGioia was hovering at his side. "Would you care to join us?" Senior college administrators and faculty had a special box next to the entrance to Healy.

"Thank you, but no. I prefer to keep out of it for now."

"But you organized it."

"But it's not my experiment anymore. In another hour it's going to be a popular experiment. For me to stage-manage it would be inappropriate."

"They'll need your help once they get inside."

"They won't get it then, either. As of now, I am logistics only."

"You're going to let them work it out for themselves?"

"If a legislative body is going to have any credibility, it's going to have to be able to stand upright on its own before it's entitled to tell others where to stand." Instinctively, Soren looked east to the Capitol, now mired in scaffolding.

DeGioia followed his glance. "Thinking about how many members of the real Congress need a wheelchair or a cane in order to hobble to their own swearing in?"

"That. And yet another advantage of the Parallel Congress. Think of the military power concentrated in that square down there, both for show and for use. Tens of thousands of soldiers and police and spies, with cameras in the sky and Fort Meade listening to every word spoken within a mile. All that force--why?"

"As a security measure."

"Euphemism and nothing more. Why?"

"So no one tries to kill the President, or the President-Elect, or a member of Congress."

"Exactly. But most people are not suicidal."

"Isn't that why a massive show of force works?"

"You misunderstand me. That it is necessary for the American government to protect itself so thoroughly is a testimony to how it stands apart from the people. Americans think about killing their leaders not only with an absence of restraint, but with outright pleasure and satisfaction. But if those leaders were drawn from the people, killing one of them would not seem either murderous or justified--it would seem like killing a part of oneself. So in the case of a truly popular government, all security could be dispensed with. Because most people are not suicidal--or genocidal, perhaps--and would be far less likely to kill one of their own."

"Don't let the Secret Service hear you say that. You'd be putting a lot of people out of work."

"The Secret Service has already figured it out. Do you see that girl over there? Your eleven o'clock, red jacket, stocking cap? She's one of theirs."

"You're kidding."

"I can see two other operatives in the crowd now, and I know that at least ten were assigned to this event."

"Do they think we're breeding insurrection here?"

"That is precisely what they think."

DeGioia mumbled something inarticulate and began to move on. "I'll speak to Justice Souter about it. By the way, he wants to meet you afterwards. Lunch?"

"I'd be delighted. After I tease the press a bit."

"Good." The president of the university departed. Soren thought about making the Secret Service agents and watching the college crowd all but dismember them, but decided against it.

In the distance, a lone voice began cheering. The spectators looked, realized that something was happening, and took up the cry. A bus edged its way slowly up O Street, turned, and came to a halt at the curb.

"Just before eleven," Soren remarked, unheard, as he consulted his watch. "And now it begins."

All over the United States, television and computer screens blinked as the networks switched from the pablum of a choir droning on in front of the Capitol to the Georgetown campus. The first member stepped out--the little old lady from Oklahoma, Soren recalled--name of Proctor. Behind her came fifty others. Behind them came ten more buses.

They filed up the one path across Healy Lawn that had been left clear. A few of them had been interviewed persistently by now, the ones who seemed likely to make better--read more controversial--copy. Most had not. Their faces showed disbelief, sorrow, joy, apprehension, confusion, eagerness, arrogance. But they moved ahead regardless, shrouded in applause and cheers. They learned quickly that it was not intimidating; far from it, that they could draw power and strength from it. In bars and on college campuses, in shelters and barracks and suburbs and in the Oval Office itself, they were watched, and for an instant the witnesses became aware of the vast energy that Soren had so carelessly tapped.

That moment passed. Then the members-to-be were filing by DeGioia one at a time, being greeted by him and handed off to Justice Souter, late of the Supreme Court, who had been prevailed upon to oversee the ceremony. They filled the benches, making themselves comfortable. The last member was seated; the last bus pulled away and bystanders surged in to fill the empty space.

A band borrowed from the Third Infantry Regiment, the Old Guard, struck up the national anthem. Their playing filled Soren with quiet glee.

He had put in a request for their presence six months ago. When it had come out that he wanted them for the swearing-in of the Parallel Congress on the same day as the presidential inauguration, the Pentagon had gone into hysterics. But by then the colonel commanding the regiment had already approved the request and made the necessary arrangements, and in due course the Defense Department was forced to bow to public pressure and allow the band to appear. The rest of the regiment would be lining the parade route about now, standing in the cold while professional politicians whom the soldiers despised made speeches over their heads. Soren was well aware that the dichotomy would be noted and commented upon. He lived for such distinctions.

President DeGioia made a very brief set of introductory remarks. Soren had challenged him to break the two-minute welcome and he came through with flying colors. Then Justice Souter, in black robes, swept out in front of the bleachers. Six hundred men and women stood up in unison.

"Raise your right hands, please," Souter instructed. "Now repeat after me: I...do solemnly swear...that I will support and defend the Constitution of the United States...against all enemies, foreign and domestic...that I will bear true faith and allegiance to the same...that I take this obligation freely...without any mental reservation or purpose of evasion...and that I will well and faithfully discharge the duties of the office...on which I am about to enter...so help me God."

The last whispers of the oath died away into silence. No one was quite certain what to do next. DeGioia returned to the microphone again.

"Citizens of the United States," he said, "I give you your Parallel Congress."

And the screams from the crowd made the stones of Healy Hall tremble.

In a little while, Soren found himself outside the audience, around the corner where the news crews had set up. One cameraman was shaking his head at the noise. "What's there to get so worked up about?" he asked rhetorically.

"They are excited," Soren said, startling him, "because they are rediscovering something that countless humans through the ages have learned and then forgotten. That government is not a thing, but an idea. That it is not contingent upon a building, or a ritual, or ancestry, or place or time. It is a human thing, which mankind can make or unmake with a single cry."

* * * * *

"How much are you paying Georgetown for this?"

"A bundle," Soren said without hesitation. That got a laugh from the reporters. "But they are giving me a volume discount as well, which helps."

In the distance, guns were going off to celebrate the presidential inauguration. No one in Georgetown cared. The newly sworn members of the Parallel Congress were being lunched luxuriously by the faculty and assorted dignitaries at a special spread across the street in the library. They had even been joined by two real congressmen, who had pointedly ignored the invitations sent to them by their own Joint Committee on Inaugural Ceremonies. No doubt there was fury in the House, or would be when Congress went into session again, but for the moment their approval ratings were the highest in the country. It pays for a politician to be seen to bow to the will of the people.

In the meantime, the crowd that had gathered watched attentively as Soren gave his first press conference since Selection Day on the steps of Healy Hall. The atmosphere was cordial, helped by the generous dispensing of liquid refreshments for which the project had arranged. Soren himself had a steaming glass of mulled wine in one hand, defying yet another American political norm.

"How did you get Justice Souter to preside?"

"I have no idea. I had one of my associates ask him. I suppose he thought it would be an historic moment."

"There are those who would say that the real history is being made down there." The journalist who made the remark nodded her head in the direction of the Capitol.

"Ah, yes, very historic indeed. If you're in a distinct minority. With voter turnout at barely fifty-four percent, and with the new President having collected a staggering forty-eight percent of that, that's a mandate consisting of less than a quarter of the total population. History, perhaps, but being made for the wrong reasons."

"Never have so few given so unclear a mandate to such littleness?"

"Yes. Excellent line. I'd say you may attribute it to me, but the cameras won't let you. Curse this modern age!" The audience grinned.

"But coming back to the subject of Justice Souter," the journalist who had originally asked about him persisted, "can it be argued that since the Parallel

Congress was sworn in by a sitting federal judge, that they indeed have the authority to make laws?"

"I'm afraid you're fishing for a conspiracy theory in the wrong place. Ordinarily the members of Congress are sworn in by the leader of each house. But the Parallel Congress has no Speaker or president pro tempore yet, so that was out of the question. If we followed the precedent of the very first law passed by the First Congress, which dealt with exactly this contingency--you'll find the text in 1 Stat. 23--then one member of each house would have sworn in the leader of that house, and the leaders would have then sworn in the other members. But that brings us back to the fact that those officials have not been chosen, since the Parallel Congress has not yet convened. So it was simpler--and, I admit, more dramatic--to have a retired Supreme Court justice administer the oath, since that is ample to fulfill the Constitutional requirements. It is clear from law and precedent that members of Congress acquire their legislative authority through election, as the first members were able to pass laws before taking any oath. The mere fact that the Parallel Congress was sworn in by a federal judge does not affect their legal standing."

"But if the Constitution were amended, they would become legislators through the act of selection instead?"

"Of course. The oath is secondary."

"One thing that your proposed amendment didn't include was a provision to set congressional pay equivalent to the members' private incomes prior to their selection. Are you paying them that much, and if so, is it enough for them to meet their expenses?"

"It should be sufficient. It won't be nearly enough, mind you, for them to dine regularly at DC's best restaurants like their Capitol Hill counterparts, or take long vacations on the taxpayer's dime. The project has leased a number of apartments in DC and Virginia and is making them available for free to members of the Parallel Congress. And they get small expense accounts as well. The University is providing them with shared office space, and hundreds of students have volunteered to serve as interns and provide secretarial help. It's quite a workable system, for now. In a perfect world, members would serve out of a sense of duty and receive no salaries at all, nothing but expenses to cover their costs. As Grover Cleveland was fond of saying, public office is a public trust. Who except a con artist seriously expects to make money out of public service? The selection system underlines that point even more forcefully. Any citizen--in theory--can be called to serve, and if they accept the call, they are merely doing their duty. Duty is less than duty if it is profitable. But that won't be practical for most people, so to make the Parallel Congress function, we have to pay them a living wage. As for their exact rate of pay, I believe that the typical member receives something along the lines of thirty-seven thousand a year, which is slightly above the national average for personal income. I attribute it to the fact that we had to build our own database by going door-to-door. That skewed our selection pool in favor of those with higher incomes. The total salaries for both houses for a year are a shade less than seventeen million dollars. Whoever predicted that the experiment would fail on financial grounds was thinking in terms of the real Congress's inflated salaries--which come to just under a hundred million dollars a year. We couldn't afford that. And neither can the United States."

"That brings us to the question of demographics. You've talked a lot about how much more representative the Parallel Congress will be than the real thing. Now that the members have been selected and sworn in, how does the final makeup of the institution compare with that of the elected Congress?"

Soren sipped at his drink and sighed in pleasure. "There can be no clearer demonstration of the differences between the American people and their elected representatives than the comparison you are asking me for. Since we were talking about salaries a moment ago, let's look at the question of comparative wealth first. More than half the members of Congress are millionaires. That line was first crossed back in 2012 and the number has gone up every year. The Parallel Congress, on the other hand, contains precisely twenty millionaires out of six hundred members, or slightly more than three percent."

"Won't that mean that the Parallel Congress will vote for more welfare programs?"

"I have no idea. That was one of the questions this experiment is expected to answer. If I knew, I wouldn't have already blown a small fortune on trying to find out."

"Hey, no offense," the reporter said.

"None taken," Soren replied equably. "As to the other discrepancies...I find it difficult to decide where to begin. The Parallel Congress differs from the Congress in almost every aspect of its demographics.

"Gender is perhaps the most visible of these areas. The Congress that was sworn in over there today"--he made a sign to avert the evil eye in the direction of the Capitol dome--"is nineteen percent female. The female members of the Parallel Congress number three hundred and three, more than half, which is understandable given that fifty-one percent of the American population is female.

"Equally clear is the age difference. While a bunch of reactionaries with canes and oxygen tanks are staggering into the marble halls across the way to devise new and subtler schemes for abusing their constituents, the Parallel Congress shows on its rolls one hundred and two members--seventeen percent--who are under the age of thirty. The real Congress? Not one. Another thirteen percent are between thirty and thirty-nine. Compare that with three and a half percent in the real Congress. By contrast, fully a third of their members are in their sixties. Ours? Under ten percent. The average member of the Parallel Congress, like the average American, is twenty years younger than the average congressman."

"But that will change everything!"

"It should be very entertaining," Soren conceded. His words were contradicted by the way he nearly wriggled with amusement.

"What about ethnic and racial groupings?"

"Less dramatic change than in other areas, as under the present system of elections, districts with large populations of minority voters often elect minority legislators. Slightly more than twelve percent of our members are black, compared to eight and a half in the sitting Congress. Members of Asian or Pacific Islander descent doubled from two and a half to five percent. The most significant shift is among Hispanics, who make up sixteen percent of the Parallel Congress as compared to seven percent of the elected Congress. I could point out that under the amendment we are using, only US citizens are eligible for selection, but those of you from Fox News are already wetting yourselves in terror of the illegal immigrant threat, so why bother?"

"Does an increase in Hispanic representation make the Parallel Congress more Catholic?"

"Actually, one of the effects of random selection is a reduction in the number of Catholics in Congress, from thirty-one percent down to twenty-five."

"That seems odd."

"Not when you consider the population as a whole. Roughly half the members of the Parallel Congress identify as Protestant, a slight decrease from the real Congress. Muslims, Hindus, and Buddhists are represented about equally in both institutions. However, the elected Congress seats twice as many Mormons and five times as many Jews as are found in the general population."

"If every religious group is more prominent in Congress, what makes up the difference?"

"You just answered your own question. Atheists and agnostics. They number fifteen percent of Americans--and thus of the Parallel Congress--but a tiny two percent of the elected Congress. To underline the point, clergymen are seven times more common inside Congress than they are outside its hallowed walls. I'm sure that tomorrow morning, talk show hosts across the nation, particularly in Texas and the Midwest, will be screaming that the godless do not deserve to have a voice in government. Associated Press and Reuters, please copy the next time one of your columnists wants to run a hit piece on why this project is anti-democratic. What could be more democratic than giving people who are reviled a voice?"

"What other professions does the Parallel Congress tend to exclude? Lawyers, obviously."

"Ah, lawyers! The Parallel Congress includes three. I have every hope that they will be ostracized, but something tells me I'm being too optimistic."

"And the elected Congress--"

"Is about forty percent lawyers."

The press broke into spontaneous applause. Someone whistled approvingly. Soren bowed, beaming.

"You see? We have already given Americans something to be grateful for: an effective means of keeping attorneys off government welfare." That got him another cheer. "One of the other great occupational gaps is teachers and professors. The Parallel Congress counts half a dozen; the elected Congress, ninety. Perhaps that will get theory out of American education policy for the first time in a century. A smaller but more interesting difference is the number of farmers, who are five times more common in the real Congress. I can only suppose that in rural states, a career in the fields makes one attractive to voters, who retain a powerful cultural image of the self-sufficient man working the land. Additionally, doctors, nurses, and policemen are all found four times more frequently downstream than they are in the Parallel Congress."

"The big difference here is laborers?"

"Correct." This time Soren's pointing finger was an accusation. "Sixty percent of Americans, and of our members, are blue-collar workers. Workers. People who do things. People who build things. People who create things. Virtually no one who took the oath of office at the Capitol today has ever done anything constructive for humanity. They are overwhelmingly talkers and schemers who are useless outside the narrow postindustrial professions they have practiced all their lives. They are trained carefully and expensively to think that they have a right to be in charge. With this attitude, they are the ones who choose to run for office, and because they have the right background, and know the right people from their upbringing, they get the nominations of their parties, giving the people no real choice when it comes time to cast a ballot. I repeat what I said two months ago. You are one hundred and five times more likely to find a Harvard graduate in Congress than in the general population. There is not a single one in the Parallel Congress, and only three members who attended an Ivy League school. The Congress that will shortly convene a few miles from here will include eighty-five Ivy League graduates in its ranks. Forty-five of these attended Harvard. How's that for being representative of the great American public!"

A low hissing noise came from the crowd. The reporters were momentarily silent, digesting the monolithic nature of the opposition that Soren was facing--and that they would be facing if they featured his statements too heavily. Soren downed the remainder of his drink and tossed the glass away.

"The remaining discrepancies are smaller and less compelling, perhaps, but they are no less revealing of the alien nature of the elected Congress. Three dozen of our members were born outside the United States, twice as many as the real Congress counts. Who will make better foreign policy, someone who has lived abroad, or someone who has never left his home state? Thirty members are either naturalized citizens or the children of naturalized citizens, compared to six in the elected Congress. Who will make better immigration policy, someone who has experienced the immigration process firsthand, or someone whose total knowledge of the difficulties involved comes from an ass-covering report written by a junior INS bureaucrat? Forty-nine members of the Parallel Congress have served in the military; one hundred and seven members of Congress have done so. Who will be more inclined to spend the taxpayers' money on useless technology and call for the erosion of civil liberties in the name of national security: the civilian, or the career soldier with friends and connections at the Pentagon and a tradition of higher allegiance to the state behind him?

"Random selection is not only more democratic than elections, it's safer, and it produces a far broader range of experience than can ever be achieved by a group of self-selecting Narcissi who went to the same schools, worked for the same firms, and professed the same fundamental belief in their own merit and in their right to make decisions for others."

"And now what happens?" a journalist finally asked.

Soren drew a deep breath. "Now," he said, "the Parallel House must elect a president."

* * * * *

Five hundred members of the House processed slowly up the aisles of Gaston Hall. From one side of the stage, the painted eyes of Athena, goddess of wisdom, watched them without comment. Wood and gilding and rich colors rose around them in every direction; the light of the winter sun filtered through stained glass to evoke the smell of aged varnish from the seats and paneling. On the stage, a temporary rostrum had been erected, perfectly in harmony with the remainder of the furnishings. A clerk was already in place to record the minutes of the House. Though smaller than the House Chamber in the Capitol, Gaston was altogether a finer room.

The gallery above the chamber itself was filled to capacity with press and spectators. A third were students who had been chosen by lot, and another third were local residents or visitors to Washington who had won their tickets in a drawing organized by the University to promote the project. In the center was a single reserved seat. Soren settled himself into it, enjoying the whispered remarks of those who had drawn positions near him, and prepared to be entertained.

The members found seats and quieted down, waiting for someone to tell them what happened next. A few, Soren recalled, had experience with city councils and school boards and such meetings. One--one!--had served in a state legislature. The rest were ignorant of parliamentary procedure, save for what they had gleaned from skimming the *Congressional Record* and watching C-SPAN for the last two months. He shivered with delight.

The House Sergeant at Arms came down the aisle, followed by a volunteer bearing an exact replica of the House mace, an ebony fasces with an unhappy eagle balancing precariously atop it. This was deposited to the right of the Speaker's chair. Then the Sergeant at Arms opened one of the doors behind the stage, and Justice Souter emerged, still wearing his robes. He took the chair and consulted a printed instruction that had been placed on the desk for his assistance.

"At present, this House has convened without a Speaker or a Speaker pro tempore," Souter began without any preamble. "This places us in a unique, although not unprecedented, situation. Before any Speaker can be elected, it is necessary to consider the special circumstances under which the election must take place.

"The intent of the Parallel Congress Project is to establish not only a Parallel Congress, but a complete and functioning parallel government of the United States, to serve as an example to the sitting government of the nation. To that end, it must select a chief executive as well as legislators.

"The language of the Twenty-Eighth Amendment affects only the election of members of Congress. It does not alter existing Constitutional requirements for election to the office of President of the United States. However, a parallel electoral college does not yet exist, nor has any election for the presidency been conducted. Therefore, a Parallel President cannot be chosen by the usual method.

"Under the terms of the Presidential Succession Act, should there be neither a President nor a Vice President, the Speaker of the House shall resign his office and assume the presidency. Therefore, when you cast your votes for the Speaker, you will, in actuality, be casting them for the future President.

"I would remind the honorable members that, while the Constitution specifies that the House shall elect a Speaker, it nowhere requires that Speaker to be a member of the House, or of the Senate. It lays down no qualifications at all for the position. The choice of the Speaker is solely your prerogative. You may choose one of yourselves, or, given the high office that the first Speaker of the Parallel House will be required to fill, you may select an experienced or inexperienced outsider you deem worthy of that office.

"The Speaker first elected shall nominate a Speaker pro tempore, and shall then resign his office. The Speaker pro tempore shall then oversee the election of a permanent Speaker for this House.

"The chair will now receive nominations for the office of Speaker."

Justice Souter leaned back in the chair and watched the members. A few of them began to confer with others in whispers. Most contented themselves with glancing around, waiting for someone else to make the first move. One minute passed. It stretched to two, then three.

A man near the rear of the hall stood up.

"Yes?" Justice Souter said invitingly.

The man swallowed visibly. He was young, lean, with close-cropped hair.

"Curtis Rodney, Emporia, Virginia."

"The chair recognizes the gentleman from Virginia."

Congressman Rodney was barely twenty, it seemed. "Mr. Justice Souter, I nominate General James Mattis for the office of Speaker."

The gallery buzzed. Soren clicked his tongue admiringly. "Trust the Marines to be first into the breach," he murmured.

"How can you tell he's a Marine?" the girl next to him whispered.

"Isn't it obvious?" It wasn't to her; she stared at him blankly before returning her attention to the action on the floor. Rodney's move had broken the deadlock.

"The chair recognizes the gentleman from California."

"Mr. Justice Souter, I nominate Condoleezza Rice for the office of Speaker."

"The chair recognizes the gentlewoman from Massachusetts."

"Mr. Justice Souter, I nominate Dr. Lawrence Lessig for the office of Speaker."

The litany of call and response went on. Soren tallied the names. Over a dozen already. Anyone whom the member putting forward the nomination happened to like or respect, or thought would do a decent job in the office. A Texan tried to nominate George Walker Bush and was silenced by the furious cries of outrage from his colleagues. Then someone tried to be clever by putting Tom Hanks into the running. The gallery laughed itself silly, but Souter allowed the nomination to stand, with an expression on his face that indicated he was beginning to regret his participation in the experiment.

Finally, when there were twenty-eight names in contention, the suggestions dried up.

"Are there any further nominations?" Souter inquired. The room remained as silent as an echoing hall containing seven hundred and fifty people can ever be. "No? Are you sure?" he queried in a rare display of judicial levity. "Then the nominations are now closed."

"Finally!" someone in the rear of the gallery hissed. Soren chuckled.

Souter was consulting his instructions again. "The rules of the House require that the Speaker receive a majority of all votes cast, excluding abstentions. Should a Speaker not be elected on the first ballot, the vote shall be repeated until a nominee receives a majority. The clerk will now call the roll."

Soren slipped out of his seat and left Gaston Hall.

"How's the vote going?" his old pursuer from the *Post* asked him over coffee an hour later.

"I have no idea."

"You aren't watching?"

"To hear them call five hundred names over and over again? That's a sure recipe for inducing nausea. What are political bloggers supposed to be for? Summarize the tedium and give us a digest of what happened."

"Then you think it's going to take a while."

"If it's settled today, they have greater stamina than I gave them credit for."

"Well, they actually have a vested interest in putting some effort into it."

"You're coming around to my way of thinking already, and it's only been a single day."

"Democracy is messy," the *Post* man said.

"Oh, you noticed?"

"I'm being serious. If there are no backdoor deals, nothing can be streamlined. Everything has to be fought out on the House floor."

"While the country watches, yes."

"I suppose the Parallel Congress has to follow the laws that already exist?"

"Of course. The idea is to give the experiment an air of continuity."

"That's going to cause problems when they try to modify existing laws and realize how tangled and interconnected the whole legal system is."

"You mean it will show off how many restrictions and limitations there are? Bring all the underbrush out into the open and burn it? Good."

"What happens, say, if the Parallel Congress legalizes marijuana, period, and then someone who's arrested for smoking goes into court and says that their Congress made it legal, so the court doesn't have jurisdiction?"

"Then the real Congress will have to address the question of what legitimacy is in a democratic society. Because by definition, whichever government the majority of the people supported would be the legitimate government. And it's about time Americans started giving some thought to serious questions again. They seem to think all the big issues have been resolved and details are all that's left to quibble over. They do this with everything, not just government. Take evangelicals, for example. All they do is argue the interpretation of single verses from the Bible these days. But fifteen or sixteen centuries ago, what were rival groups of Christians arguing over? The very nature of Christ's divinity! The big question to end all big questions. Men's minds have gotten small. The Parallel Congress will stretch them again."

"Like a shoe?"

"A vivid image, but not inaccurate."

"What did you think of the Hanks nomination?"

"I seem to recall that he was once voted the most trusted man in America. But that was years and years ago."

"So he'll get it?"

"Possibly, but not entirely likely. Besides, there's the question of acceptance. Whoever the House elects has to accept the office, and I somehow doubt one of the century's biggest film stars is going to take a couple of years off to participate in a social experiment bound to be heavily criticized."

"That's not in the Succession Act or the Constitution."

"But it's implicit in any election. Even the Pope, who is chosen by the Holy Spirit moving in men, has the right to decline his election."

"Condoleezza Rice, then."

"Also possible. High approval ratings, but she's been out of active politics for a while."

"Gives her a good platform to come in as an impartial elder."

"Whom many of the members of the Parallel House may not have heard of before today."

"Who do you think it will be?"

"When it all works out in the first round? My guess is Robert Gates. High approval ratings, known moderation--and very little known about his specific views."

"That could work against him, too."

"Of course. And who knows if he would give up the presidency of his alma mater to play the Parallel President in my little multi-dimensional chess game. Although he detests the real Congress. Think back to the ire at them he's expressed in his memoirs for their incompetence. He might accept the position as a form of delayed revenge. To show that normal people with a sane man at the helm can govern better than professionals."

"What about Neil deGrasse Tyson?"

"He'll appeal to the environmentalist crowd, but you can't forget that a substantial minority of the people in that room think he's a liar and a cheat out to oppress them. Will that scuttle the nomination? It could depend entirely on the order of the balloting. If he looks unlikely early on, his more pragmatic supporters will probably switch to someone else. If he retains some support into the final rounds, he's got a chance."

"In other words, there's no way to tell."

"As you said, democracy is messy. But which is more stimulating, not to mention entertaining? Trying to pick one winner out of two possibilities, when a poll already tells you which one of them is more likely to triumph, or trying to pick one winner out of twenty-eight possibilities?"

"Some of us like a simpler choice."

"We could always amend the Constitution so that the Electoral College followed the Venetian model for electing the president."

"What was that?"

"Thirty legislators picked nine of their number by lot, the nine elected forty, the forty were narrowed to twelve, the twelve elected twenty-five, the twenty-five were narrowed to nine, the nine elected forty-five, the forty-five were narrowed to eleven, the eleven elected forty-one, and the forty-one elected the doge."

"Enough! That's madness!"

"Mad, possibly, but it also worked well to guarantee that the head of state would not be chosen on the basis of bribery or political games, since predicting the outcome was effectively impossible."

"Greater complexity in government isn't a solution that would recommend itself to many Americans." The *Post* reporter wrapped his scarf back around his neck and stood up. "Thanks for the history lesson. Anything else my readers should know?"

"Oh, yes," Soren said. "You can remind them that the longest-serving member of Congress has been there for forty-eight years. How's that for responsiveness to the will of the people?"

* * * * *

Balloting for the office of the Parallel Speaker took two full days and eight rounds. As Soren had predicted, it went to Gates in the end by a fair margin. The former Secretary of Defense dithered for three days and then declined, citing his skepticism towards the experiment.

Justice Souter sighed and began the balloting process all over again. This time the number of nominations was down to nineteen, giving some hope that the Parallel Congress might be able to elect a President by the end of the month if all went well. Lessig ruled himself out of the running by talking too much about how the Parallel Constitution could be reformed. One social experiment at a time, the members decided, was challenging enough. An experimental constitutional convention on top of an experimental government would be too confusing to handle. Condoleezza Rice went fully GOP and condemned the project, ensuring the withdrawal of her nomination. Also eliminated were a librarian from Mission Viejo and a cook from Michigan.

A pro-Sanders faction was gently turned down by the still-serving senator, who made it clear, though not in so many words, that he was not willing to give up real legislative authority just to set an example to his former rivals. A pro-Ron Paul faction failed to interest the majority of the House and fizzled out.

Then the members began to get annoyed. Every attempt they made to reach out to elder statesmen, former senior officials, retired legislators, and prominent activists was being rejected. Sometimes the rejection took the form of a public denunciation of the project by the figure in question before the Parallel Congress had even thought of approaching him. Soren's prediction that no professional politician or activist would support the experiment, because its success would risk closing off their access to power for good, was borne in upon the House with a force they had never anticipated.

Out of sheer pique, its members closed ranks. On the second ballot of the third round of voting, they elected the owner of a drugstore from a small town in Idaho. No one really knew anything about his politics, but they knew him. He had been prominent in trying to broker deals among the various groups that were emerging in the Parallel Congress. When nominated, he almost shouted his own nomination down, but was tugged back into his seat by his friends. After the vote, he hesitated and finally mumbled his acceptance in a voice so low that it deprived the watching cameras of the sensation they were anticipating.

"It is worth noting," Soren said when asked for comment, "that seventy percent of Americans view pharmacists as being highly ethical and trustworthy. Only nurses are seen more positively. Members of Congress, on the other hand, are trusted by exactly eight percent of the population."

"So you wouldn't have been surprised to see a nurse elected?"

"Not at all. We have half a dozen currently serving."

"Do you think this is what the country can expect from the Parallel Congress in the future?"

"If you mean unexpected decisions, then yes, absolutely. Anyone who has ever looked--actually looked, rather than trying to find support for their preconceptions--at what Americans think about the issues will find that their collective desires fit none of the accepted patterns. You are in for some shocks over the next two years."

Fighting back the beginnings of a midwinter cold, and with a glint in his eye that said he anticipated returning to his books as soon as this tedious business was over, Justice Souter informed the druggist that the presidency was vacant and that, under the terms of the Presidential Succession Act, he was next in line. The new Speaker appointed a Massachusetts fisherman as Speaker pro tempore and resigned his seat in the House. The Senate, which had been cooling its heels in the library all this time, with nothing much to do until the framework of the government was established, squeezed into the gallery of Gaston Hall to observe the inauguration. Souter administered the oath of office to a shell-shocked Chief Executive and promptly left.

"It's not very grand, is it?" a student at the back of the hall said.

"It doesn't need to be grand," her neighbor replied. "This is going to be a hell of a lot of work."

The Speaker pro tempore immediately opened the balloting for a replacement Speaker. Three names were placed in nomination. A union leader from West Virginia was elected on the very first round.

Soren was eating a salad in O'Donovan Hall, surrounded by admirers, when a House page turned up with a note for him. He read it in five seconds and handed it back. "The answer is no."

"That's it, sir?"

"That should be sufficient."

The page had his trip for nothing. He was sent back at once with a second note. Soren's response was the same as before.

The Parallel Speaker waylaid him outside the cafeteria and demanded a better answer. "After all, you brought us here. You set up the system. No one knows it like you do. No one is better qualified to serve as the returning officer for the House. So why do you keep declining?"

"Because," Soren explained patiently, "I am going to great lengths to remain entirely independent of this experiment. You must work it out for yourselves, without direction from me. I will observe, but I will not participate. While I understand that you intend this offer as a form of recognition for my efforts, anyone intelligent could do the job. I decline absolutely. And you'll thank me later on, if the public ever starts calling the selection process tainted, since I will have averted that for the time being by staying out of it."

"So we appoint one of our own, then?"

"For choice you should select an outsider. A non-politician. Someone for whom it's just a job, not a public service."

The Parallel House eventually decided to hire a professor from the University's mathematics department who had done interesting work in game theory. As the Speaker explained to the press, it was thought that someone obsessed with the purity of numbers would be the safest choice to oversee the selection of new members.

The returning officer brought another randomly purchased computer into Gaston Hall. Mr. Brewster arrived from the project's lawyers with the database and the returning officer entered the necessary command to determine who was to fill the House seat vacated by the Parallel President, who had been required to resign in order to assume the presidency. The name was read out, the Speaker phoned the selectee and confirmed that he was willing to serve, and the House applauded politely.

An hour later, the press went wild when it was determined that the new member of the Parallel Congress was a neo-Nazi from North Dakota. Soren, confronted with the resulting public revulsion, shrugged it off.

"Granted, that does give them a disproportionate voice, but these things happen with randomization. Next time it could be a member of the Communist Party. Now that would make for some fireworks on the floor of the House, since Nazis and and Communists are one another's mortal enemies. Democracy is inherently discordant. And in any case, the argument can be made that both the Democratic and Republican parties are fundamentally national socialist in their views as it is."

"But how did this guy get into the database in the first place?"

"I have no idea. We made a point of not asking people about their political views when recruiting them."

"Shouldn't there be a process for the Parallel Congress to expel a member?"

"There already is. Article One, Section Five of the Constitution. It needs a two-thirds majority."

"Think it will happen?"

"We'll see. If it does, it would set a highly dangerous precedent, to be expelled for being unpopular rather than for misconduct. The beauty of this system is supposed to be that even the most marginalized views are represented. They have to be if a legislative body is to be truly, comprehensively democratic."

*****

The *Post* reporter slipped into the vacant seat beside Soren in the gallery. "What did I miss?"

"They just voted on a bill requiring the budget to be balanced."

"Was it a fight?"

"The debate lasted fifty-three minutes and the bill passed with eighty percent support."

"Damn. Congress must be writhing in agony right now."

"The public has made it abundantly clear for decades that they want a balanced budget. Congress has spent the entire time laughing it off. After all, less money means less power for them. Now they'll have to take their medicine."

On the floor, a member from Maine was warming up on the subject of defense cuts.

"Now as I understand it," he was saying, "now that we've decided to make a balanced budget work, we have about five hundred billion a year in spending that we either need to cut or make up in tax hikes. Here's a simple solution: we kill the F-35 fighter program. In spite of all that Lockheed can claim for it, it's still costing more than a hundred million per plane. And the Air Force doesn't want less than fifteen hundred of them. So that's a trillion and a half dollars over the next ten years if they can get a hundred planes a year--which is doubtful, because the Pentagon is set on shoving them down the throats of our allies abroad while withholding the maintenance software, resulting in a world filled with airplanes that it controls. Soft power, they call it. At any rate, that's a hundred and fifty billion off the deficit right there without touching anything else. Just by getting rid of something we don't need that wouldn't work anyway."

"The chair recognizes the gentlewoman from Texas."

"Mr. Speaker, both my husband and my brother-in-law happen to work at the Lockheed Martin plant in Fort Worth. They are two out of eighteen thousand employees. I believe that this House tacitly agreed that reducing unemployment would be its highest priority after resolving the disaster that our budget has become. May I ask my fellow members how they can justify a defense cut that would throw eighteen thousand people out of a job? Isn't that a betrayal of our priorities? Surely we can find the financial breathing space we need simply by eliminating the waste, fraud, and abuse that accounts for probably half of government expenditure. In addition, I would remind the House that we need the F-35. The Chinese air force is currently acquiring a hundred and fifty new planes every year. Their fleet will equal ours in size by 2030. Even a hundred new F-35s a year is insufficient to maintain our strategic advantage."

"The chair recognizes the gentlewoman from Ohio."

"Mr. Speaker, it is not the job of the United States government to provide jobs for its citizens. Not unless I woke up this morning in the Union of Soviet Socialist American States. I like to think that the American economy is still strong enough that it can absorb a few thousand highly skilled workers with excellent employment records. I would also like to point out that the cost to the government, if we were to pay every worker at that plant an average of fifty thousand dollars a year for the next ten years as severance pay, would be less than one percent of the total cost of the F-35 program. It is also less than a third of what Lockheed Martin is likely to make in profits over the same period."

"The chair recognizes the gentleman from Colorado."

"Mr. Speaker, I spent several years in the Air Force sitting in a hole in the ground in charge of a bunch of nuclear missiles aimed at some unknown destination in the eastern hemisphere. I'd like to say that I don't appreciate the member from Texas reviving those old bogies of the bomber gap and the missile gap. That the Chinese air force, four thousand miles away on the other side of an ocean its fighters can't cross, should be equal to ours is not in and of itself cause for alarm. Has our fighter superiority forced us to attack them? No, we have other concerns. Therefore, it would be misguided to think that their fighter superiority would force them to attack us. The logic doesn't work. In any case, as the failure of the Star Wars and other missile defense programs demonstrated, any defensive system you construct can be cheaply overwhelmed by feeding it too many targets. Our focus in procuring defense technology should be on systems that are cheap and numerous.

"We already have an excellent fighter in our existing F-16 Falcon. Instead of throwing good money after bad with the F-35, we should go back to the best plane we ever had and reopen the production lines, making incremental changes along the way to both simplify and upgrade the airplanes. It's aerodynamically far superior to anything that the Chinese, the Russians, or NATO are fielding if only we didn't clutter it up with all the nonsense that manufacturers out for a government contract try to push on us. We supplement those cheaper planes with the new Reaper drones, which can do the air-to-ground mission far better than any manned fighter. Have you ever met a pilot who can loiter on station for thirty-six hours? I haven't. But the Reaper can."

"This isn't right at all," the *Post* man said quietly. "They're actually debating the details of the budget on the floor rather than tossing it into committee."

"Yes, it's called open government."

"It's just unnerving. I spent ten years covering the House of Representatives. Debate is basically unknown. It all goes on in small rooms and then they troop out onto the floor to vote along party lines, and that's it. This is much less ritualized than the normal House proceedings, too."

"Because these people are actually interested in the questions under discussion instead of maneuvering for advantage. Are they selfish? Of course. They're as self-interested at bottom as any elected congressman. But--they have less practice at expressing it, and the situation they now find themselves in doesn't give them time to indulge it. It forces them to focus on scoring points for cleverness and creativity in an attempt to make names for themselves as successful leaders in the two years available to them."

"The chair recognizes the gentlewoman from New York."

"Mr. Speaker, even if we accept my colleague's assertions that we can get a simplified and improved F-16 for sixty million once it's back in full production, and that we can get the Reaper drones for sixteen million, if we buy one pair of that combination for every F-35 we were going to buy, at the same rate, that only gives us twenty-four billion a year off the deficit. It's a start, but we need a lot more than that. Following the same line of thinking, to moderately reduce military expenditures, I propose that we eliminate all military aid to other nations, which costs us ten billion dollars every year. Why should we be giving aid to every country in the Middle East so they can use it to fund an arms race against each other? That seems counterproductive to me. In addition, I suggest that we trim six billion dollars from the budget for the State Department, which is about the difference between its usual appropriation and the actual cost of its operations. That would bring us up to a deficit reduction of forty billion dollars."

"The chair recognizes the gentleman from New Mexico."

"Mr. Speaker, I think we need to realize that the truth of the situation is that we can't eliminate the deficit through cuts alone. Not under the present circumstances, anyway. There are a few things we can agree on cutting: defense and government overspending, foreign aid--but the fact of the matter is that most of us think spending on most government programs should either stay the same or be increased. So that leaves us with our other option: raising taxes. A national sales tax of six percent would raise four hundred billion dollars a year. That would eliminate most of our deficit right there."

"The chair recognizes the gentlewoman from Oregon."

"Mr. Speaker, four years ago my home state considered a ballot measure that would have imposed an additional sales tax of two and a half percent on the gross sales of all businesses that had more than twenty-five million dollars's worth of sales in a year. We estimated this would generate around two and a half billion dollars a year in revenue. By extrapolation, I suggest that this tax applied to all large businesses in the United States would provide annual revenues of two hundred and twenty-five billion dollars. More importantly, this burden would fall on those best able to afford it: large and profitable corporations. Small businesses and individuals would be exempt from the tax, and large but unprofitable businesses would be forced to reform their practices or go bankrupt. It would thus provide an economic stimulus entirely apart from its benefits for our national budget."

"The chair recognizes the gentleman from Tennessee."

"Mr. Speaker, for most of the twentieth century, the top income tax bracket was far higher than it is now. For decades we saw top rates of seventy, eighty, even ninety-four percent. More importantly, there was a clear divide between what rich and poor paid. Today, the rich man pays four times as much as the poor man; in 1936, he paid twenty times as much. For sixty-three years, the highest income tax bracket was at or over fifty percent. Currently the IRS uses two top tax brackets of thirty-five and thirty-nine percent. I propose we consolidate these, and that we raise the tax rate on both to a flat fifty percent. This would bring in an additional fifty-two billion dollars a year in tax revenue, and would restore historical norms to the American tax system."

"That's a failed proposal right there," the reporter whispered.

"Oh, really?" Soren replied. "You're forgetting that this isn't a millionaires' Congress. This is a people's Congress."

"But it doesn't have to be filled with the wealthy for a tax like that to fail. There are still a lot of people down there whom that impacts."

"All that the gentleman from Tennessee just did was raise taxes on less than one percent of the population. The dividing line between the 'one percent' and everyone else is the $380,000 a year income level. That means there are about six people in Gaston Hall right now who would be personally affected by this increase and would vote against it on those grounds. Everyone else will be fine with it. You underestimate how poor and dependent the average American actually is."

"The chair recognizes the gentlewoman from California."

"Mr. Speaker, we keep talking about taxing things like income and goods, which are actually useful. Why don't we discuss taxing something that's actively harmful, like poison? Every year we pump unacceptable amounts of carbon dioxide into the atmosphere, and we do nothing but stick band-aids on the problem with grants to develop new energy sources. It's time we did something to actually cut down on the toxic waste we're creating. A carbon tax would both allow us to do this and help resolve our budget crisis. If we taxed every ton of carbon dioxide released at fifteen dollars apiece, that would raise an additional eighty billion dollars to be put towards deficit reduction. In ten years' time, it would cut fossil fuel consumption in the United States by twenty percent. More importantly, it would help us survive. And, as with my colleague's proposal for an additional sales tax on large businesses, it would force economic reform. Energy companies that sought larger profits would be compelled to phase out coal and oil and gas in favor of solar and wind energy, because doing so would be the financially smart thing as well as the ethically smart thing. We have to make the two coincide, and we can do so for the common good."

"The chair recognizes the gentleman from New York."

"Mr. Speaker, this is ridiculous. I'm not exaggerating when I say that I'm almost too shocked to stand. Instead of getting sensible suggestions on how we can cut government waste and government entitlements, all I hear is tax, tax, tax. You all don't like big business? I get that. But if that big business isn't thriving, there won't be any jobs to solve the unemployment problem. The only way to grow the economy is for employers to have incentives to hire and spend. Tax, and you take that away. If you're really interested in the common good, then it doesn't matter what we pay as individuals. The main concern is that employers should have low taxes to keep the economy moving."

"The chair recognizes the gentlewoman from Georgia."

"Mr. Speaker, I agree with the gentleman from New York that we haven't heard enough about cuts. So I propose that we slash the foreign aid budget, all forty billion of it, down to zero. We pay forty billion a year to be just about the most hated and criticized country in the entire world. We were doing a hell of a lot better when we were giving nothing away in aid and everyone wanted to be like us. You don't make friends by giving handouts. Handouts insult them. Charity reminds them that we look down on them, that we're patronizing them, that we're implying they can't take care of themselves. This Congress should learn from the mistakes our predecessors have made and get rid of its paternalism."

"The chair recognizes the gentleman from Rhode Island."

"Mr. Speaker, I have been keeping track of the numbers my fellow members have been suggesting this afternoon, and taking both budget cuts and tax increases into account, I find that they total just under eight hundred and thirty billion dollars. We have a deficit problem of five hundred billion to resolve. Clearly we are well ahead of our goal--in fact, we are doing far better than our elected counterparts ever did." Laughter from the chamber and the gallery. "With that in mind, I would like to suggest that we adopt all of these proposals with one slight revision to lessen their impact on middle and lower-class Americans. Instead of a six percent national sales tax, I propose that we institute one of three percent. Three percent will still provide us with an enormous boost in revenue and will pinch the pockets of the vast majority of consumers much less.

"That reduction still leaves us a hundred and thirty billion dollars ahead of the deficit. I would also suggest to this house that we spend thirty billion of that sum to stimulate employment. The most effective means by which we could do so is to put the money into building transit networks, and for the past decade, Americans have been showing an increasing desire for a national high-speed rail network, to the point where many now say they would prefer rail travel over aircraft or cars. Granted, national high-speed rail would be expensive: over five hundred billion dollars. But it would be a long-term project in any case. Therefore, I propose that we allot thirty billion dollars a year to such a network until it is completed, which we can well afford with these tax adjustments. By doing so, we will create an additional six hundred thousand jobs. The remaining hundred billion dollars we will reserve towards paying down the national debt, so that our children, or at least our grandchildren, will not have to carry that load as well. And I am confident that with care and application, we will be able to make enough further cuts to existing programs to considerably increase the rate at which we will be able to pay it off."

A congressman from Texas jumped up and began raving about how the income tax was illegal and un-American to begin with. The House listened politely, but without interest.

"It can't pass," the *Post* reporter said, shaking his head. "It can't pass."

"It will," Soren said as he finished the last of his popcorn.

"But how?"

"Did you ever know the real Congress to pass any piece of legislation that didn't benefit itself and its members?"

"Of course not."

"The Parallel Congress is the same way."

"You think that they think they'll benefit from this?"

"That sounds slightly involved, but in a word, no. I don't think they think they'll benefit. I *know* that they think that. Sixty-four percent of Americans think that defense spending is either just enough or too low. They won't cut it as a whole very readily, but the F-35 program is such an easy target, and when they were told they could get more bang for less buck, naturally they agreed to a small reduction. Ordinary bargaining instinct. More than half support cutting foreign aid. Half would also support a national sales tax at the six percent rate; more will undoubtedly support a lower tax. Sixty-one percent think the rich don't pay enough tax; sixty-seven percent think corporations don't pay enough tax. Fifty-six percent support a carbon tax. Half support cutting foreign aid. There are majorities in favor of every separate item these delegates proposed, and the way they have now been packaged together will make them even more appealing. The effect of these new taxes on the people in this room will be negligible. In return for such insignificant concessions as they will personally end up making, they get a balanced budget, a reduced national debt, a national rail network, a drop in unemployment, and a more powerful military. The combination is irresistible."

"Do you have a statistic for everything?"

"Yes. This entire project is built on statistics."

"And cynicism."

"Says the professional cynic."

"Let's leave personalities out of it. How do you think this will go?"

"A few dozen congressmen who still believe in Reaganomics will use up every second of their allotted time to denounce this proposal as a guaranteed failure. It may take a couple of days for them to run out of breath. Then the House will pass it without too much further fanfare."

"It's that good?"

"Good has nothing to do with it. A majority of the population would approve of it, and the Parallel Congress is a microcosm of the American population."

* * * * *

The House Committee on Energy and Commerce was in session in the Philodemic Room, an appropriate setting for one of the oldest of the standing committees. Oak paneling and nineteenth-century portraits accorded far better with the legislative spirit than the pale, brightly lit industrial offices of the Capitol where hearings had previously been conducted. The committee itself was more compact than its rival version as well. The Parallel House had reorganized committee assignments and pared Energy and Commerce down from fifty-four unwieldy members to a more manageable twenty-one. Since there were no parties in the House as yet, and thus no majority and minority whips to make nominations to the committee, they had fallen back on having the Selection Officer choose the committee members at random from the House as a whole. So far the system had performed admirably.

"Wind energy," Professor Ivers of Stanford was testifying, "is, on the whole, inferior to solar energy for large-scale applications. Wind turbines require a great deal more space than solar panels, both vertically and horizontally. They cannot be adequately miniaturized, either. You can put solar panels on the roof of your house, and that's useful, but a wind turbine in your backyard will make a much less significant reduction in your electrical usage.

Both wind and solar energy are variable, but solar is much more reliable and predictable than wind.

"In terms of expense, a solar farm that can power two hundred homes will cost about three million dollars to construct, while a wind farm with the same capacity will likely run to ten million dollars, and could be as much as sixty percent more."

"Why the combination of wind and solar in current use, then?" the congresswoman from Kentucky wanted to know. "Why both if one is better?"

"Two main reasons. First, it's taken us a lot of research and development for us to get to this point. We had to build examples of both systems to see what they were capable of. Now we know. Second, the two systems complement each other to a certain extent. Solar panels generate no energy at night, but turbines will turn twenty-four hours a day if there's a breeze. If a storm comes up, insolation drops and so will electricity generation from solar panels. That same storm will generate more energy from turbines as the wind picks up. It requires a balance."

"But solar should be the mainstay of a clean energy system."

"That is the conclusion we have come to. It has the added advantage of being easily scalable. If you want to put panels on your roof, then you can lower your own monthly energy bills. If you have a bit of land and want to install more solar capacity than you need, you can sell the excess energy back to the grid and get paid for it. It's a very low-impact, personalized solution."

"What would you say is the major obstacle to an increase in solar energy generation in this country?"

"Oh, without question, efforts by utility companies to deter consumers from installing their own solar panels. That cuts down on the amount of energy they can sell and thus on their profits. If they've made long-term commitments to purchase gas or coal years into the future, and they're not selling enough energy to warrant fulfilling those contracts, but they have to do so anyway, then it starts to really hurt them. So a number of companies have begun adding surcharges to the bills of customers who install solar generation, or raising their rates selectively. This has already been the subject of legislative action to prevent energy discrimination in several states."

"What about the cost of solar panels?"

"Dropping every year, and we expect it to continue to do so as the industry expands with growing demand."

"Is foreign competition driving prices up?"

"Actually the tariffs that are currently in place--which apply mostly to wind turbines--are designed to exclude cheaper products from Europe and China, both of which are farther advanced in renewable energy technology than the United States."

"Why are utility companies not leading the way in conversion to solar power?"

"The expense of the equipment. Take Consolidated Edison, for example. It serves three point four million customers, about one percent of the entire US population. Say one point three million households. For it to convert to solar energy would cost nearly twenty billion dollars. And that doesn't take into account that it supplies an exclusively urban area, which would mean added costs to install its solar capacity outside the city limits and add the necessary transport infrastructure."

"Consolidated Edison made a profit of four billion dollars last year," a congressman from upstate New York pointed out.

"But they'd rather keep that money. Remember, ConEd isn't a cooperative, it's owned by people looking to make money off one of the essentials of modern life."

"But my point is, they have the resources to do it over time if they want to. They could convert entirely to renewable energy by 2030, and still have room for more modest profits."

"Oh, certainly."

"And how much of an impact would a national conversion to renewables have on our air quality?"

"An enormous one. Electrical power generation is the single biggest contributor to carbon dioxide levels in the atmosphere, to the tune of two billion tons released every year. That is entirely from burning coal and gas. Vehicular emissions are less than that, at one point eight billion tons, and so we'd still have to face that problem, as well as the carbon contributions of industry, but those are problems that are less easily resolved. Fixing our electrical grid is the quickest and easiest way to fix our atmosphere."

"How do vehicle emissions break down by type?"

"Fifty-nine percent are generated by private cars. Twenty-two percent by commercial trucks. Eight percent by aviation. The remainder is from trains, ships, and alternate methods of transportation."

"How much does the fossil fuel industry receive in federal subsidies every year?"

"Not as much as you would think. About four billion dollars. There's more in the Department of Energy's budget for research, but that's mostly directed at carbon sequestration--at solving the problem rather than contributing to it."

"The previous Congress and administration touted a bill that would reduce methane emissions by five hundred thousand tons a year. Is that good?"

"Any reduction is good, I suppose."

"But not good enough?"

"The amount of methane we pump into the atmosphere is about seven hundred and thirty million tons a year. Reducing that by half a million is so ridiculous a concession that it's worse than doing nothing."

"How do we correct that?"

"The same way you get carbon dioxide emissions down: renewable electric power. Most of our methane emissions come from electricity generation."

The committee chairman looked around. No one was pressing for attention. "Professor Ivers, thank you for your time."

"Thank you."

The professor trooped out. The audience turned its full attention back to the committee.

"That was ridiculous," a member from Indiana sniffed. "This is none of our business."

"Then let's withdraw that four billion dollars going to fossil fuel subsidies. How about that?"

"Fine by me."

"Does anyone second the motion?"

"Second," Connecticut said.

"All in favor?" Twenty-one hands went up.

"Now," the member from Indiana went on, "let's put that money back towards reducing the debt."

"Or," countered California, "we could use it to electrify two hundred and sixty thousand homes every year. Either give the money out to citizens for them to use to install their own solar capacity, or build solar generation plants and give away free power."

"That's not the least bit fair! How do you decide who gets the plants or the money?"

"I admit plants would be difficult to allot, but a national lottery for a grant to install solar panels would be very popular."

"And a very great waste of tax money."

"More of a waste than paying it to the utilities so they can burn toxic substances?"

"It's a nice gesture, but an insignificant adjustment," Virginia said. "The real trick is to get the utilities off of fossil fuels."

"Letting individuals supply their own power will chip away at their dominance," Arizona put in.

"Too little and too slow. Besides, they can always retaliate by raising their rates, as the professor explained."

"Then we declaw them. Multiple states have already banned surcharges on solar users as an abuse of a monopoly. Why not make it federal? A criminal offense to exploit power consumers who are trying to do the right thing for themselves and the environment."

"Okay, so that protects consumers who want to clean up the air, but it doesn't induce producers who are polluting to do the same."

"Mandate that they convert to renewable energy."

"That's impossible!"

"It could be done in ten years, and without them even giving up all their profitability. And in the long run, solar panels will be a lot cheaper than boilers and turbines."

"No. There isn't financial room for that in the industry."

"The average electric company charges each customer for the equivalent of thirteen months' service every year, but only provides them with twelve months' worth of power," the member from Hawaii observed. "That's over eight percent profit. They can afford to make a slow switch."

"But the intrusion of federal regulations--"

"What regulations? We introduce a new Clean Air Act. We require all utility companies to convert to renewable energy by the end of 2030. We present a staggering schedule of fines for the ones that haven't complied or are deliberately dragging their feet. And that's it. Let them worry about how they do it; as our friend from Indiana keeps saying, that's not our job. As long as they do it, everyone wins."

"Additional benefits of that proposal," Illinois added, "are that the solar and wind industries will gain a huge boost from the sudden demand, with a resulting rise in employment, and that we can cut about twelve billion dollars out of the Department of Energy's budget."

"How do you figure that?"

"That's how much it spends on securing, maintaining, and inspecting nuclear power plants every year. Nuclear energy is not renewable. It won't be included in the Act. So we get another savings off that and eliminate an additional environmental hazard at the same time."

"Nuclear energy is perfectly safe."

"Except when it isn't."

"Where are we going to put the waste?" California demanded.

"Not in my backyard," Colorado added.

"Just to get a sense of where the committee stands," the chairman inquired, "how many of us would support a ban on nuclear energy?"

Eleven hands went up. The audience stirred with excitement.

"A bad move."

"A sensible move. Saves money and cuts pollution."

"Hurts the economy, too."

"Please. You really think nuclear technicians will have any problems finding jobs installing solar panels? If we replace one industrial sector with another, where's the net loss?"

"The net loss is the disappearance of critical skills and an essential national security technology."

"The national security people themselves say the greatest threat we face is the degradation of our environment."

"Nuclear power is important to our economy and our global prestige. It doesn't affect our environment nearly as much as automobile emissions."

"We already have a partial solution to reducing vehicle emissions with the high-speed rail project."

"Only if we specify that it will be electric."

"That's simple enough. But it doesn't have to be. Even a conventionally-fueled train is three to four times more efficient than cars or trucks."

"Trucks are the unseen part of the equation. There's about two million tractor trailers in the country. But they're the ones accounting for most of that 22% contribution to emissions. The problem is that they're not included in the Energy Tax Act. They don't have to meet the same kind of emissions standards that our cars do. So we amend the act to include them, as well as vans and SUVs."

"And we raise the standards. The top tier for vehicles, where they pay no tax, is only twenty-two point five miles per gallon. Why shouldn't it be thirty? If the average figure by 2025 is supposed to be thirty-four-and-a-half, a top bracket of thirty seems reasonable."

"If the rates went up to the point where a new truck warranted an additional twenty thousand in fees, and they were being replaced at a rate of about a hundred thousand a year, that's an extra two billion in taxes. Enough to make a niche industry sit up and take notice."

"Meaning that it would force a move to rail traffic, and that the trucks that did survive would have better fuel consumption anyway."

"What about raising the rates for failure to meet the CAFE standards as well?"

"That wouldn't have much impact. The only ones who ever pay the fines are luxury car manufacturers. The ones who make normal cars are already well ahead of the standard. The demand exists, so they meet it."

"The key appears to be creating a demand and letting existing industries shift to fill it."

"Then we can create a demand for recyclables as well. The United States produces more than fifty-five million tons of plastic every year and throws away ten million tons of it. About sixty billion dollars' worth. All of which has been produced from fossil fuels."

"A tax on new plastics."

"More precisely, a tax on new plastics produced from petroleum or precursor chemicals--not on those produced from the recycling of other plastics. Ten cents a pound would bite the manufacturers but wouldn't hurt the consumer, and it would bring in eleven billion dollars a year that could be used for environmental remediation elsewhere."

"And it would spark off a whole new industry. Plastic doesn't degrade. Every piece of plastic ever discarded in the United States is sitting in a landfill somewhere. If we've only averaged five million tons a year for the last fifty years, then that's fifty billion dollars in taxes producers could avoid by recycling those deposits."

"Self-sufficiency in plastics?"

"It could be possible."

"At the risk of destroying well-established business practices."

"That's the idea," California snapped. "Companies either start treating the environment right and being more efficient, or they go bankrupt."

"The message to businesses is clear," Colorado concurred. "Fix this, or you will pay for it or even go to jail. This isn't a game. This isn't about making money. This is about our health and our survival. If you're going to make us sick and try to defraud us, you're going to pay the price."

*****

"The chair recognizes the gentleman from Delaware."

The Parallel Senate was in session beneath the elegant paneled roof of the Bioethics Research Library, at the opposite end of Healy Hall from where the House was deliberating. Outside, it was a warm spring, made warmer by the way the library was packed to capacity. The floor was entirely filled with chairs and desks for the senators, and the gallery, with its Victorian-style brass rails, was standing room only. There was no space for seating. At each corner, a camera peered down onto the floor, where the soft afternoon light spilling through the porthole-like windows illuminated the heavyset man clambering to his feet.

"Mr. President, I rise to ask that the Senate do something that it should have done long ago: debate and consider the National Health Care Act originally introduced in the House.

"For seventeen years our predecessors sat on this very reasonable piece of legislation and ignored it. Too expensive, they said. Too invasive, they said. And then we got the individual mandate, which has been a disaster and nothing but a free gift to insurance companies. So I propose that we replace it altogether with the single-payer healthcare system that the majority of Americans want, or that they would at least prefer to the cumbersome mess of the ACA.

"Americans spend two and a quarter trillion dollars on medical expenses every year. Four hundred and seventy billion dollars of that represents the administrative costs of our existing payment system. Clinics and hospitals and labs all talking back and forth to one another, and all talking to multiple insurance companies. Insurance representatives wading through files to see whether your particular prescription at your particular doctor will be something that they have agreed to cover, or whether they're going to make you drive across town to get it filled. Of course, in such a system, there's no incentive for them to simplify. The greater the complexity, the greater the number of employees they need to manage it all; the greater the number of employees they have, the bigger the bottom line of their company and their prestige. Not to mention their profits. The more work they pretend to do, the more they can charge you.

"A single-payer healthcare system would end all of this rivalry and purposeful overlap by consolidating medical payment processing into a single government agency. There would be no disputes over coverage, because everything would be covered. There would be far less misplacement of paperwork, because it would all be centralized. It would put economy of scale to work for consumers rather than against them. Even if the NHCA only reduced administrative costs by half, that would save the average American six hundred and fifty dollars a year, or two thousand dollars per household.

"Administrative savings are not all we can expect. The NHCA cuts medical expenses even further by prohibiting participating institutions from operating on a for-profit basis. It would result in the eventual conversion of nearly all hospitals and clinics into nonprofits. I will offer just one example of how this will help consumers. The average hospital visit lasts four and a half days; the average hospital makes a profit of about one thousand dollars from that stay. If all hospitals were nonprofits, your bill would be lower by that thousand dollars. The effect of this provision is to return medicine to its roots as an altruistic service to the community, not a means of making a fortune.

"The NHCA will be paid for by a combination of higher income taxes on the top five percent of wage earners--similar to what our colleagues in the House have already proposed--a small tax on the trading of stocks and bonds, and a payroll tax to which each of us will contribute just as we would to Social Security. Its demands will not be onerous, and any increase we see in the amount of taxes we pay each year will be canceled out by the absence of any premiums or out-of-pocket costs that we will have to pay for medical insurance or care.

"Now, I am aware that some of my fellow senators are ready to start screaming that this is socialized medicine. And I would like to remind them that it's nothing of the kind. We have no intention of taking over hospitals and running them; that would be an administrative nightmare that would create worse problems than the ones we're trying to solve. This changes nothing as far as the practice of medicine itself is concerned. The only thing it changes is who pays the bill. Instead of you making payments at high interest to an insurance company for years at a time, you take a small deduction on each paycheck and never have to worry about paying any medical bills. The government handles the rest as a public service, and that's what government is there for, isn't it? For those of you who say this is exploitative, I say it's less exploitative than allowing private corporations to make profits off our pain."

"The chair recognizes the gentlewoman from Nebraska."

"Mr. President, this bill is an unacceptable intrusion into the private lives and finances of Americans. It places an undue burden on the average taxpayer to constantly be subjected to a deduction for medical care regardless of whether or not he needs medical care. If it turns out that he doesn't, then he's subsidizing someone else's expenses. He's being forced to give away his earnings to someone careless enough to have gotten hurt. If we have the state telling us that we must pay for medical care, soon it will also be telling us what operations we can have or what doctors we can see, no matter what we think about that. This legislation would also place an unfair and unbalanced strain on wealthy individuals, who are thereby forced to foot the bill for the weak and the indigent. It is contrary to everything in the American public spirit, which encourages citizens to succeed in business. It is fatal to entrepreneurship, to initiative, and to freedom."

"The chair recognizes the gentleman from Utah."

"Mr. President, I find the remarks of the distinguished senator from Nebraska to be short-sighted and deliberately callous. I grant that if you are never going to need medical care, then a payroll tax to support a healthcare system is a way of subsidizing someone else's care. However, the truth of the matter is that virtually everyone will need medical treatment at some point. One out of every two people in this room will be diagnosed with cancer, more or less serious, sometime in their lives. And that's not including heart disease, vehicle accidents, or the biggest killer of all: simply growing old. If we all pay into this system, it is because we will all use it. As for the worn-out complaint that the wealthy will be carrying the indigent, that is to define everyone in this country who doesn't make a six-figure income as indigent and unworthy. The top five percent of income earners are those who make more than a hundred and seventy thousand dollars a year. If their extra share of the NHCA tax is an extra one percent, that's seventeen hundred dollars, which means a lot less to them than three hundred would to someone making thirty thousand a year. The former isn't going to get evicted because of that one percent; the economic situation in this country is such that the latter very well might if he had to pay it."

"The chair recognizes the gentlewoman from Oregon."

"Mr. President, this discussion of how to provide adequate medical care is overlooking what should be a vital aspect of our national healthcare policy: prevention. New treatments and research programs are important to that, of course, but they should be only a minor portion of a much larger emphasis on good health to begin with. While I support the NHCA enthusiastically, its financial impact on all of us would be much less if a third of us weren't obese." She glared around at her fellow senators, some of whom were noticeably straining the capacity of their chairs. "Or if, as the senator from Utah said, we were not prone to heart disease and cancer and vehicle accidents. Any sensible approach to healthcare policy must include a means of increasing physical fitness and improving diet. Or a single-payer system will eventually fail for the reason that there are no taxpayers left to pay into it, because we've all eaten ourselves to death. Therefore, I propose that any health care reforms we make include a tax credit for those who can demonstrate that they are in excellent physical condition and thus less likely to place demands on the system."

"The chair recognizes the gentleman from Alabama."

"Mr. President, this bill does not address religious exceptions. I must express, in the strongest possible terms, that as a taxpayer I would resist it violently if it did not. And so would the vast majority of Americans. We will not pay unjust fees to enable a slut to kill her child or a queer to stay alive."

"The chair recognizes the gentleman from Colorado."

"Mr. President, I've had it up to here with people creating problems by begging for exemptions and then doing nothing to solve those problems. The senator from Alabama doesn't want to pay for abortions--but I'm willing to bet that he also doesn't want to do something useful to make them unnecessary. At home, we have a program to provide publicly-funded contraception. In the first four years, it dropped the abortion rate thirty-five percent and saved us five dollars in Medicaid funding for every dollar we spent on it. And that's a low measure of its potential. Nationally, it would probably reduce the abortion rate by forty-one to seventy-one percent. It would also save the healthcare system eleven billion dollars a year by preventing a million unplanned births. No violence, just common sense. It's the right thing to do, and the economical thing to do, and it should be part of the NHCA."

Twenty senators were on their feet, clamoring for attention. The Vice President of the United States, restored under the Parallel Congress to his original role as President of the Senate, gaveled frantically for order.

"Delicious, delicious," Soren purred from the gallery.

"Do you ever plant questions or ideas in their heads just to see the reaction on the floor when they trot them out?" the *Post* reporter asked sharply.

"I don't need to. They come up with this all on their own. Isn't it wonderful?"

"It's a headache for the rest of us who have to make sense out of it. Although I am impressed with how involved they are. I didn't think the American population was so politically conscious."

"You'll notice, as time passes, that only a small fraction of the members will actually be contributing ideas to the conversation. Those who were already activists, or passionately concerned with a particular issue, will lead the way and make most of the speeches. The others will vote and speak based on what they learn in this chamber from those who go first."

The debate, or rather the series of polemics, dragged on. Senator after senator rose to denounce the idea of doing anything at all to reduce the birth rate on ethical grounds. Their statements grew increasingly acrimonious. Under the eyes of the spectators, they were very aware that they were not doing justice to their cause. A few, emboldened by their sense of hostility, declared straight out that all forms of interference with reproduction should be prohibited and Americans allowed to fill the earth with their offspring without restraint.

Then one of them made a mistake and accused the federal government of attempting to practice mind control through contraceptive drugs, which brought roars of laughter from the gallery and diverted the direction of the proceedings.

"The chair recognizes the gentleman from Montana."

"Mr. President, the position was just advocated that the government should not be dispensing drugs. I am not going to comment on that at present--as I understand the bill which we are debating, it contains no provisions that the government will provide medical care directly--but I am going to point out a related factor in the healthcare equation that we have been ignoring so far. The issue of paying for healthcare would be much more easily addressed through drug legalization. That would save the federal government fifteen billion dollars a year through reductions in the number of people jailed on drug charges, and it would also stand to benefit by collecting some or all of the forty-six billion dollars in tax revenue that could be raised through the sale of legal drugs. Advocates of marijuana legalization tout its potential as a source of income, but marijuana would only be responsible for about eight billion of that. The lion's share would come from the legalization of cocaine and heroin. And that is in estimated tax revenue from sales alone. The economic impact of bringing the entire trade out in the open, creating jobs and businesses, would lessen the burden of any additional taxes imposed to pay for a healthcare system."

"The chair recognizes the gentleman from New York."

"Mr. President, the legalization of dangerous drugs is not an option. If, in the interests of raising money to keep ourselves healthy, we make something unhealthy available to the public, we are accomplishing nothing. I agree that it is time to end the half-century of waste we have come to call the War on Drugs. I agree that mandatory minimum sentencing should be abolished, and that treatment should take priority over imprisonment, but putting heroin back on the streets in misguided allegiance to a principle of personal freedom is not the right way to go about ending both government and public abuse of controlled substances."

"The chair recognizes the gentlewoman from California."

"Mr. President, I would like to ask the senator from New York exactly how he defines a dangerous drug. What is the fatality rate that he considers to be evidence that a particular substance is a threat to public safety? Because if we are going to keep drugs like LSD and magic mushrooms on the banned list, when neither has ever been documented to have caused a death from overdose, I propose we amend the NHCA to also prohibit alcohol and tobacco, which are collectively responsible for nearly six hundred thousand deaths every year."

"And here we go," Soren murmured as the Senate descended into chaos.

* * * * *

"It occurred to me," the *Post* man said, "that the Parallel Congress, if you kept it going, could easily come to serve as the real government of the United States."

Soren yawned and took a mint from an elegant antique snuffbox, beautifully decorated with gold filigree and opals. "Are you off on the popular mandate angle again? That sovereignty will transfer automatically when a majority of the population switches its allegiance?"

"No, that angle has been worked to death already. I was thinking of something simpler and more informal. No legal change at all."

"Enlighten me."

"It's an easy switch. The real Congress falls into desuetude--"

"You could argue that it already has."

"--and because of its great age and the convoluted nature of the processes in which it has trapped itself, it stops making laws altogether. Members hear their constituents and air issues, but they don't actually introduce bills or debate them. They wait for the Parallel Congress to make a law, and then they approve it as a matter of course. The actual legislative process would take place here, and the real Congress could fund it as a non-governmental organization. No need to alter the Constitution or the integrity of existing institutions. Custom and practice would be all that was required."

"In short, you are proposing an equivalent to the British constitution, where nothing is written down and practice and precedent hold sway. There's no law that says the monarch cannot veto legislation, but it hasn't been done in three hundred years. There's no law that establishes the office of prime minister, but in practice that title is given to the head of the Cabinet. The Magnum Concilium still exists as a parliamentary body in theory, but has not met in four hundred years."

"Something like that."

"It would invalidate the part of the experiment that was supposed to make the government less cumbersome."

"Speaking of which, when are they going to get on with this hearing?" The Hall of Cardinals was a grand but not spacious setting for the Senate Judiciary Committee, whose eleven members were packed behind a narrow table against the far wall. The portraits of robed churchmen of a past century leered down at them, providing an appropriate ambience for the forthcoming interview of a Supreme Court nominee, the third that the Judiciary Committee would undertake. Two appointments to the Parallel Court had been confirmed already. Today's choice was expected to involve much more of a fight and public interest was accordingly high.

"Any time now. The chairman is sorting through the agenda."

"Do you think the President picked a nominee who was too conservative to pass the Senate's scrutiny?"

"It's hard to tell. A small plurality of Americans prefer their Supreme Court justices slightly conservative. The Court, after all, is supposed to provide stability and ensure fidelity to the Constitution."

"I suppose we never really know anyway until they actually get on the court. Most turn out to be something of a surprise once they start hearing cases."

"If they start hearing cases even then." The reporter raised an inquiring eyebrow. Soren elaborated. "Take Clarence Thomas, for example. He hasn't actually heard a case in, what, twenty years? He falls asleep the second he clambers onto the bench."

The journalist half stifled a raucous laugh. "And to think that the *New York Times* once called him the most activist justice on the Court."

"Pretty generous for someone whose main activity is snoring."

At the end of the room, the Judiciary Committee chairman gaveled for order. "This hearing on the confirmation of Judge Charles Elbert

Lindemann to the United States Supreme Court is now in session. Judge Lindemann, welcome."

"Thank you, Madame Chairman."

"As a rule," the senator from Florida continued, "these hearings traditionally open with the honorable members of Congress lying their heads off about how well-disposed they are towards the nominee and reassuring him that they have every confidence in his good character and abilities. In the interests of saving the public's time, we are going to skip the pontificating and the self-serving statements and move right to questioning the nominee. Do you have any objections to raise, Judge?"

"None whatsoever. I welcome the Senate's sense of urgency."

"Excellent. There are no lawyers sitting on this committee, which means that we will appreciate you keeping your responses directed towards the issues that our questions raise, rather than the intimate details of cases and opinions we are not familiar with. To begin with, Judge, I will ask what your position is on the constitutionality of the War Powers Resolution."

"The War Powers Resolution was authorized by Congress under the terms of the Necessary and Proper Clause of the Constitution. The Constitution, it is reasoned, gives Congress the authority to maintain the armed forces; therefore, Congress has a share in directing how those forces will be used, as it is authorized to make laws governing how the powers of the entire government, including those of the presidency, will be carried out. It requires the President to report on the state of ongoing conflicts to Congress in order to determine if he is acting within the limits of his authority. This ostensibly conflicts with the manner in which the Constitution allots the role of Commander in Chief to the President. For Congress to regulate his performance of his duties by law risks overstepping the boundaries between the legislative and executive branches."

"The committee is aware of the conflicts involved in the law as it currently stands. What we are looking for is a statement on how you would intend to rule on the constitutionality of the resolution, particularly in a case where it had been demonstrably ignored by the President."

"Well, I would like to point out that every report submitted to Congress under the terms of the War Powers Resolution has used the language that it is 'consistent with', not 'pursuant to' the resolution. The executive branch has never formally admitted that the War Powers Resolution is binding, although it has never challenged it in court. The last four presidents have all engaged in military actions that might be regarded as evading the requirements laid down by the resolution, and they have a reason for doing so. There is a compelling government interest in preserving national security, even when the details of that interest are the subject of valid legislative and popular debate. Under those circumstances, the President may consider that he is justified in acting without the benefit of Congressional oversight, and may expect that Congress will eventually support him, as indeed it has in the majority of instances where this discrepancy has arisen."

"In other words, you would find the War Powers Resolution unconstitutional if you were to hear a case involving it."

"I am afraid I cannot comment on a hypothetical situation that might well arise during any justice's term on the Court."

"Do you consider the President to be bound more by the law, or by the interests of the nation?"

"The President must weigh the interests of the nation against the laws as they currently stand, and endeavor to bring about the repeal of those laws that conflict with the best interests of the nation."

"Ah, but who determines what the best interests of the nation are? The President? Congress? The Supreme Court? Or the public?"

"In general, I could not advocate for the primacy of any one source in the interests of maintaining the best possible relations between all three branches of the government and the citizens of the United States."

"Let's be specific, then. When it comes to a military situation, who is best placed to determine the best interests of the nation?"

"As the Commander in Chief, the President must take the lead. The Constitution makes that clear."

"Does the President's determination overrule that of Congress?"

"The President should work with Congress to find a solution that is acceptable to both."

"Should? Not must? What if no solution can be reached?"

"In that case, Congress must either trust the President's judgment or impeach him for abuse of his office. When threatened, our nation must respond to that threat with the clarity and direction of a single voice. That is why the Commander in Chief is an individual, not a debating body."

"This is getting interesting," the *Post* said under his breath.

"He's a real judge, you know," Soren replied. "Retired, but very real all the same. A professional. He's not being nearly as cautious as he would be before the elected Judiciary Committee. He looks down on these average American senators. Contempt breeds candor. Behold the power of democracy, to strip away the fraud of office!"

The chairman gaveled for silence and frowned in Soren's direction. Then she nodded at one of the other committee members.

"Judge Lindemann," the senator from New Hampshire began, "the decision of the Court which has provoked the greatest public outcry in recent years was that in Citizens United v. Federal Election Commission. Do you regard that decision as an appropriate application of the First Amendment?"

"The jurisprudence of the Citizens United decision is quite clear. The First Amendment protects speech by associations as well as by individuals. That an association should be formed primarily for the purpose of making a profit rather than for a more altruistic cause does not deprive it of its right to free speech. As the opinion itself made clear, 'There is no such thing as too much speech.' As concerned citizens, we should welcome the intrusion of new views into our political process. As men and women living under the rule of law, we should respect the way in which that law preserves rights even to those with whom we disagree. Just as importantly, Citizens United is a reassertion of equality under the law. To allow some institutions, and not others, the privilege of freedom of speech would be as unconstitutional as denying freedom of speech to all associations."

"But is an association entitled to rights to begin with? An association or an institution, be it a corporation, a nonprofit, a political advocacy group or a dogwalkers' union, is a concept. It is not a person. Do concepts have legal and civil rights, or only individuals?"

"The legal system of the United States has long accepted that such entities do have legal and civil rights. If they did not, they could not function. American law regards corporations, associations and institutions as compacts formed by multiple individuals in order to express themselves collectively as a single individual. Congress is the highest form of such a compact. They are given standing as legal persons not by statutory law, for there is no statute that defines them as such, but by our desire and need to regard them as individuals with whom we may interact on our own behalf. Their existence is ratified by democratic consent, and so are their rights. And since we regard them as persons, it would be a violation of the Fourteenth Amendment to seek to deny them rights equal to those of any other individual."

The senator from Minnesota consulted his notes and leaned forward. "Judge, you have just given us a fervent defense of First Amendment rights. In the case of the American Civil Liberties Union v. National Security Agency, the Sixth Circuit held that the ACLU did not have standing to sue the NSA because their belief that they had been targeted for government surveillance was insufficient to prove that they actually had been targeted. However, the state secrets privilege prevented them from subpoenaing NSA records to prove or disprove their contention. This strikes me as a catch-22. They cannot sue without standing, but they cannot demonstrate standing without proof, and they cannot obtain this proof without suing. Does not such a decision have a chilling effect on First Amendment rights, in that it provides an inducement for individuals to curtail their First Amendment activities lest they inadvertently expose themselves to surveillance and find themselves unable to obtain judicial relief?"

"It is well established that there is a compelling government interest for the federal government to carry on surveillance programs within the parameters laid down by Congress. It is also not well established that the individual is in any way harmed, or can expect to be harmed, by being made the subject of surveillance. If they cannot show that they have been injured by the attention of a government agency, then they have no cause for obtaining judicial relief, and if they freely choose not to speak or write out of a misguided fear that it will cause the government to watch them, that is a decision for which they, and not the United States government, are responsible. Actions protected by the First Amendment could not be prosecuted by the government in any case, so the decision of the Sixth Circuit is well-founded."

"You fail to address the issue that perhaps the only reason why an individual cannot show he was harmed by surveillance is because the records of that surveillance are not available to him. If someone is blackmailed by an NSA employee based on information that employee discovered during legal surveillance, how can he--or the prosecuting attorney, for that matter--demonstrate harm without access to the NSA's records?"

"Well, that's an improbable hypothetical which I think any court would reasonably rule was less important than concealing information which could compromise national security."

"Judge Lindemann, this is not hypothetical. As established by General Dynamics v. United States, the state secrets privilege has been expanded to allow courts to dismiss cases altogether on the grounds that merely proceeding would compromise national security. This is an obvious contradiction of the right to a fair trial established in the Sixth Amendment, and specifically of the Compulsory Process Clause."

"I believe that the wording of the Sixth Amendment specifies a speedy and public trial, with an impartial jury. Nowhere does it mandate that the government is required to hold a trial; rather, whether or not a case is proceeded with is within the discretion of a particular court."

"That does not explain away the Compulsory Process Clause."

"As the Court laid down in Taylor v. Illinois, the public interest may sometimes be allowed to override the Compulsory Process Clause. The right is not absolute."

"Do you consider that such a position makes you a loose constructionist?"

"I have always prided myself on a faithful adherence to the written text of the Constitution in any situation where I was required to consult its meaning."

"So not very often, then," Minnesota said. Lindemann did not respond to that remark.

The senator from Nevada took up the gauntlet. "Seven years ago, in Navarette v. California, the Court held that an anonymous tip may justifiably become the basis for police action if the police deem that tip to be reliable. They considered the case in relation to the probable cause standard of the Fourth Amendment. They did not consider it in relation to the Confrontation Clause of the Sixth Amendment. Since an anonymous tip by its very nature does not permit the accused to be confronted by his accuser, should Navarette be overturned?"

"There are no grounds for thinking that it should be. The accusers in Navarette were the police officers who made the arrest, not the tipster. They duly appeared in court and gave their testimony, and the accused and their representatives had the opportunity to cross-examine them at that time."

"With all due respect, Judge, that's a lawyer's evasion. The officers who stopped the truck observed no illegal activity until after they did so. The ultimate cause for that stop, and for two men going to jail, was the testimony of an unsupported, anonymous source. Whether the complaint was thought to be reasonable or not was irrelevant. The case should have been thrown out for failure to produce someone who could actually have given a reason for the defendants to be stopped in the first place."

"With all due respect--Senator--that is a fair and accurate application of the law as it stands. There is no compelling reason that witnesses should be placed in jeopardy in order to provide defendants with a totem for their resentment. There was ample evidence in the Navarette case to secure a conviction, and the tip provided probable cause. The production of the caller was unnecessary."

"Except for the fact that the proceedings were tainted as a result and a principle of justice that has endured for two thousand years was tossed aside. What about Tupper et al v. City of St. Louis, where the Missouri Supreme Court struck down an ordinance permitting red light cameras? Does not the use of such cameras also violate the Confrontation Clause? The camera is not a person, so it cannot confront the accused."

"The camera, however, is not legally the accuser. The accuser is the officer who reviews the footage from the camera and generates the ticket for the violation."

"But a clerk in a back room at the police station would not have any idea that a potential violation had been committed without the input, after the fact, from the camera. The camera is the prime mover, but it is not an acceptable witness."

"The camera is merely a tool used by law enforcement. The officer who writes the ticket is responsible, and the Confrontation Clause is upheld by his appearance in court with the necessary evidence."

"Evidence of such a nature that its creator cannot be interrogated to determine whether the evidence is truthful or false. The testimony of a police officer in such a case is effectively hearsay. The letter of the Constitution might be upheld by that, but not the spirit."

At that point the hearing began to grow acrimonious.

* * * * *

Soren looked out the window of his office at the Capitol dome, and the little legislators and aides rushing about beneath it. The trees on the National Mall were bright with the new greenery of spring. The cherry blossoms were back again.

One of his staffers slipped into the room and quietly closed the door behind him. "You have four very unhappy people downstairs who want to see you."

"I expected that. Send them up."

A few moments later, his guests filed into the office. Burton Chesney, Republican, stocky and scowling; Jacob Cardozo, Democrat, tall and suave with the unmistakable air of the successful attorney; Petros Mikhail, Libertarian, with a phone in one hand, a radio in his ear, and Google glasses that were recording every second of the meeting; Annette Barbour, Green, former beauty queen turned animal rights activist.

"We have a problem," Chesney led off, not waiting for Soren to greet him. "Well, two problems actually. The second and more urgent of which is why, when I asked for a private meeting with you, you set up an appointment for me at the same time as these characters."

"I'm sure we'd be happy to give you the chance to have things out with Mr. Soren," Cardozo put in, attempting to start the conversation more amicably. "However, since the rest of us are here as well, the question becomes: who gets to have it out with him first?"

"None of you." Soren said flatly. "I set all of your appointments for the same time--with considerable difficulty, I might add, you were so uncooperative--because I intended for you all to be here at the same time. Are you aware of why I chose to do so?"

"To annoy us?" Chesney bellowed. Mikhail contented himself with a shake of the head before returning his attention to his phone. Barbour viewed them both with distaste, their shoes in particular.

"In part," Soren said with the direct honesty that had made him the darling of the American public. "Also because it will be more instructive for all of you. And it will save me having to explain myself four times over, which I find very tedious.

"Those, however, are explanations of motive, not of fact. The factual reason for your presence is that you have all, unknown to each other, contributed a fair portion of the funding that is keeping the Parallel Congress operational, and you want an accounting of it. You are, to put it mildly, dissatisfied with the laws that the Parallel Congress is passing."

"Wait--we all contributed?" Cardozo said in alarm. Mikhail put his phone away and began paying attention.

"Did you suppose it would be cheap to teach the United States government a lesson?"

"You never told us," Barbour complained.

"Number one, if you had been aware of the additional sources of funding, you would have been willing to donate less. As things currently stand, we have enough committed funds from all of you in reserve to keep the project running for the full two years no matter how unhappy you are with its results. No welshers allowed. Number two, you were all required to sign agreements that you would never disclose your participation in funding the experiment while it was ongoing, in order to prevent members from coalescing and forming party networks around you, their benefactors. Number three, if you had been aware that by donating you were climbing into bed with your rivals, you would have all backed out."

"So you cheated us," Cardozo said.

"On the contrary, I gave you exactly what I promised in return for your money."

"It's not what you promised!" Chesney snapped. "It's--it's--" He floundered, unable to find the phrase that would adequately express his outrage.

"What would you like me to do?" Soren asked sweetly. "To lean on the Parallel Congress? To influence its members from their random impartiality in order to produce results that are more Republican? Or Democratic? Or Libertarian? Or Green?"

"You said it would," Barbour reminded him. "You told me that a people's Congress was bound to produce results that were more environmentally sound than one composed of professionals with a stake in the destruction of the environment."

"I told you the literal truth. I told the same thing to all of you, in different variations, and every time it was true. The Parallel Congress has passed bills that all of your parties would have liked to see become law--except that it has done so on their own merits, and not in conjunction with the rest of your platforms.

"And that is what you four have against me. You expected the Parallel Congress to vindicate your own views completely. To give you something to which you could point as evidence and declare, 'The majority of the Great American People agree with me!' You are all independently wealthy outliers in your own parties, who don't like party discipline and think a drastic shakeup is just what the American political system needs--provided that it occurs in your particular direction. You backed the Parallel Congress, intending that its results, unrigged, would serve your purpose. It was a purely selfish move for all of you. Oh, I freely admit that I encouraged you in your selfishness, if only for the lesson in contrasts it now provides.

"For instance"--he pointed at Chesney and Cardozo--"you two are horrified that the Parallel Congress killed the F-35 program, with all of its pork and potential for overseas aggression, but you two"--here he indicated Mikhail and Barbour--"are perfectly happy about that.

"Three of you are furious that they raised taxes. Two of you resent that they cut foreign aid. Chesney and Mikhail don't like the rail program. Chensey and Cardozo don't like cutting the fossil fuel subsidies. Nobody but Barbour likes the entire solar energy program. Chesney and Mikhail hate the new vehicle emissions standards and the National Health Care Act.

"They pissed you two off by passing an assault weapons ban and universal background checks, and they pissed you two off by passing a national concealed carry system. *You* were so busy shouting that Americans love guns, and *you* were so busy shouting that they hate guns, that you all failed to notice that they like some guns and dislike others, and want their own but just don't trust certain people with them. The distinction was too fine for your polemical minds to grasp.

"Chesney is having fifty thousand fits about them providing a path to citizenship for illegal immigrants. Cardozo, Mikhail, and Barbour are all unhappy that they banned refugees. Mikhail and Barbour can't stand the new tariffs and trade regulations. Their approval of GMO labeling has upset everyone but Barbour. Chesney and Cardozo are up in arms about them approving a constitutional amendment to abolish the Electoral College and determine the presidency by popular vote. Chesney is not pleased that they ended the draft once and for all. Cardozo and Barbour don't like the new requirement that welfare recipients will be required to prove employment to receive benefits. Chesney and Cardozo are both comfortable with the fact that military spending has hardly diminished under the Parallel Congress, while Mikhail and Barbour are disappointed. Barbour basks in the glow of the ban on nuclear energy and fracking. She joins Mikhail in applauding marijuana legalization, while Chesney and Cardozo are quite put out about it. Chesney and Mikhail are tearing what little hair they have left over the new minimum wage, while Cardozo and Barbour find it acceptable.

"You all got some of what you wanted, but far from all of it. Now, if you believed in the old trope that politics is compromise, you might find that a bearable situation. But you don't. You are all here because of your naivete. You truly believed that if the government only asked the people, they would agree with you. That your ideology was their dearest desire if they could come to express it.

"Well, they got their chance and they failed you. It must be quite a shock to the system. For you four, a working government is one which puts your principles into action. But the mob has no principles, only an instinct for what they think serves them best. They do not strive to reshape society to an end; they endeavor to reduce the demands that it makes of them. I gave you a perfectly balanced, ideally representative legislature. And, by your standards, it's not working."

Mikhail was the first to break the silence. "Since it's not working, as you say, what do you suggest we do about it?"

"Since none of your competing factions can agree on a method of government, and since the alternative of popular government is unacceptable to all of you? Abolish government."

Chesney made a strangling noise in his throat. Cardozo's lips had disappeared in anger.

"That was really the whole point of this experiment, wasn't it?" Barbour asked.

Soren chuckled and held out his snuffbox to them. It was filled with tiny pills of a lovely translucent green.

"Opium?" he inquired. "For the masses. To help you cope with them."

Also by this author:

Hyperdrive

L'Affaire Famille

Totum Hominem

The Bettor

In the Name of God, the Merciful, the Compassionate

Ships of the Desert

The Senator Dies at Dawn

A Case of Impiety